More Scholastic titles by Malcolm Rose

Breathing Fear

Circle of Nightmares

The Smoking Gun

Plague

His immune system was despatching every weapon at its disposal through the narrow crimson tunnels of his body to confront the surging viral armies. From his lymph nodes to his liver, white blood cells engaged in running battles with the rapidly growing hordes of the rampaging virus. Very soon, his defence would be outnumbered and outwitted. It had never seen such an enemy before and it had no way to combat the threat. It had never learned how to deal with such an invader. His throat was filling with lymphatic fluids. Unseen, blood had begun to seep into his lungs.

When it was Jessica's time, when she yelled her third obscenity and the baby's head appeared ——————————— er's eyes were not ——————————— brain was muddled. ——————————— hideous alien's he ——————————— e, cruelly tearing her apart. He shook with a sudden chill, uttered a cry of horror and collapsed.

More Scholastic titles by Malcolm Rose

The Alibi
Breathing Fear
Circle of Nightmares
Concrete Evidence
Flying Upside Down
The Highest Form of Killing
Lawless & Tilley: The Secrets of the Dead
Lawless & Tilley: Deep Waters
Lawless & Tilley: Magic Eye
Lawless & Tilley: Still Life
Lawless & Tilley: Fire & Water
Lawless & Tilley: Lethal Harvest
Lawless & Tilley: Flying Blind
The Malcolm Rose Point Crime Collection
The OBTUSE Experiment
Son of Pete Flude
The Smoking Gun

Tunnel Vision,
Winner of the Angus Book Award 1997

Point

Plague

Malcolm Rose

■SCHOLASTIC

Scholastic Children's Books,
Commonwealth House, 1-19 New Oxford Street,
London WC1A 1NU, UK
a division of Scholastic Ltd
London ~ New York ~ Toronto ~ Sydney ~ Auckland
Mexico City ~ New Delhi ~ Hong Kong

First published in the UK by Scholastic Ltd, 2000

Copyright © Malcolm Rose, 2000

ISBN 0 439 01013 6

Typeset by
Cambrian Typesetters, Frimley, Camberley, Surrey
Printed by Cox and Wyman Ltd, Reading, Berks.

4 6 8 10 9 7 3

For Kirsty Skidmore
who reacted so strongly to this novel

Plagues are as certain as death and taxes.

Dr Richard M. Krause, US National Institutes of Health, 1982.

The survival of the human species is not a preordained evolutionary program. The single biggest threat to man's continued dominance on the planet is the virus.

Joshua Lederberg, winner of the 1958 Nobel Prize in Physiology or Medicine, Rockefeller University, 1989.

The world has rapidly become much more vulnerable to the eruption and . . . global spread of both new and old infectious diseases. The dramatic increases in world-wide movement of people, goods, and ideas is the driving force behind globalization of disease. A person harbouring a life-threatening microbe can easily board a jet plane and be on another continent when the symptoms of illness strike. The jet plane itself, and its cargo, can carry insects bringing infectious agents into new ecological settings.

The world needs a global early-warning system capable of detecting and responding to new emerging infectious disease threats to health. There is no clearer warning than AIDS. Now we ignore it at our peril.

Jonathan M. Mann, François-Xavier Bagnoud, Professor of Health and Human Rights, Professor of Epidemiology and International Health, Harvard AIDS Institute, 1995.

The agent of botulism food poisoning is too small to be seen with the naked eye, yet a twelve-ounce glass of the toxin it produces would kill every human being – all 5.9 billion – living on the face of the Earth. As small as germs are, they rule the world.

As a human race we are facing the greatest public health disaster the world has ever known.

Barry E. Zimmerman and David J. Zimmerman, microbiologists and identical twins, 1996.

Chapter 1

Yombe sat on the edge of her father's bed, looked into his crimson eyes, and cried tears as clear and colourless as water. The liquid that trickled down her father's cheeks from his blood-filled eyes was deep red.

She could not even hold him. He recoiled in agony at the slightest contact with his skin. His nerve endings were on fire. A sheet, a hand, clothing, everything tormented him. The disease denied him – and denied Yombe – the comfort of touch. The lining of his throat was too sore to allow him to utter words or to drink water. The side of the bed was black with the blood that he had vomited. His face and neck bulged outwards with the pressure of accumulated blood and fluids. Most of his hair had fallen out and clumps of it clung to the folded blanket that served as a pillow. His wasted head looked like a sickly bird lying in a dishevelled nest and his breath smelled of decay. Occasionally his body writhed and quaked like a dog having a fit. Other times, he would lie unnaturally still as if death had taken pity, but in fact he was simply exhausted.

The medic could not explain it. She knew only that the tiny capillaries that carried blood from this man's arteries to all parts of his body were overflowing like the stream after the rains. Just as the river pushed its surplus water into the fields, woods and sometimes into the village, his capillaries were discharging their overload. He was leaking blood. But she didn't know why. In a respectful but matter-of-fact whisper, the nurse told Yombe that she expected him to die within a day or two. And, no, nothing could be done. All of her white medicine could not stop a river in flood.

Until the torture stopped, until the illness had utterly ravaged its victim, Yombe could only stay in the hut, watch and talk and hope that her father could see through his red curtain and hear through blood-caked ears.

Ngoi stood outside Yombe's home and

recited the traditional prayers, keeping away bad spirits. While the white nurse tended Yombe's father, the priest would not enter the hut because the two of them had clashed over the coming funeral arrangements. Ngoi would visit the sick man only after the outsider had left. Then he would dispense his own magic and medicine. Yet his doctoring was as futile as the nurse's.

Yombe was torn. Not only was her father dying but she was being tugged in one direction by native tradition and in the other by white ways. Her instinct told her to obey the priest that she had known all her life – the village expected it of her – but her reason sided with this peculiar English woman who had come of her own accord to help a community that she wasn't part of. She was tending to strangers. And that impressed Yombe. The white woman could have washed her hands of the affair and walked away from it. But she didn't. She stayed. She cared. Besides, sixteen years ago, Ngoi had not been able to save Yombe's mother as she screamed with the pain of a bad labour. In giving Yombe life, her mother had sacrificed her own. Yombe was a first and last child. She had never forgiven Ngoi.

*　　　*　　　*

Really, Heather Caldbeck was a midwife. Her knowledge of childbirth and hygiene was her passport throughout Africa. In Zaire she was delivering important messages about cleanliness, contraception, safe sex and obstetrics in Yombe Embale's village when the girl's father succumbed to a mysterious disease that Heather had no hope of curing. She wasn't trained for it. At first, she guessed that he had an infection. It wasn't malaria. On her travels she had seen plenty of malaria – sometimes resistant to drugs – and knew that Yombe's father was suffering from some other illness. Desperate, Heather tried to convince herself that he might have contracted a particularly destructive strain of malaria that she had not seen before so she gave him chloroquine. That way, she was at least doing something. But, as she expected, there was no improvement. The treatment did not even slow down his deterioration. If it was an infection, it was moving through his body like a larva flow, engulfing and burning everything in its path. Whatever it was, it seemed merciless. Once she had given him nivaquine, every antibiotic that she had, aspirin, cardiac stimulants, blood coagulants and vitamins, she ran out of ideas and drugs. She didn't have the weapons – or the knowledge – to combat the disease. All she could offer was sympathy.

Heather was certain, though, that he would die. She guessed that his tremors would lead to a full-scale seizure or his heart would stop because of the loss of blood. Either way, the result would be the same. Not so much death as release from the illness. Yombe's father would welcome it.

She had also fallen foul of the people's culture. When a man of the village died, it was the custom for the women in his family to clean the body – externally and internally – with bare hands and then bury him beneath their hut. Then, the family was thought to be protected by the purified man. Heather warned them against this tradition. She was not driven by repulsion. The ritual would be distasteful to her Western eyes but she was driven more by concern for the village and for Yombe in particular. The girl was her father's only relative. She was the one who would have to delve into her father's diseased body. If he had an infection, Yombe would be exposed. And the burial custom would add to the risk of spreading it. Only a thin clay floor would separate his body, possibly riddled with microbes, from Yombe and any visitors to the hut. With her own home, Yombe would become a very desirable mate in the village. If she took a man and started a family, they would be endangered, not protected, by the corpse of Yombe's father.

Heather had tried to persuade the priest that, once Yombe's father died, his body should be touched only with hands in surgical gloves and that it should be burned well away from the community. At the very least, he should be buried in a cemetery outside the village. But she'd failed to move the old priest and change the old ways. Ngoi had been offended and hostile. In tangling with tradition, Heather had succeeded only in alienating herself from the people. Her influence in the village had decreased almost to nil. Yombe herself still invited Heather into her hut to tend to the dying man.

Yombe and Ngoi were bilingual. They spoke Bantu and African-dialect French – sometimes a curious mixture of both. They also had a smattering of English – learned from the charity workers and missionaries. Heather did not speak Bantu but her French was passable. She used French, occasionally sprinkled with English, to make herself understood. When spoken language let them down, they relied on the international language of arm-waving and facial expression. When she'd explained that their death ritual should be changed for the sake of the villagers' safety Heather did not need to know Bantu to understand Ngoi's response. His angry tone and violent gestures were perfectly eloquent.

Near the end, Yombe's father lay absolutely still as if he had gone beyond pain, as if his body no longer reacted to it. When, finally, he escaped the dreadful clutches of his disease – and of his devastated body – Yombe looked to both Ngoi and the nurse. Their different stands, their different demands, had not changed. They could not agree. It was up to Yombe to choose.

For Yombe there was only one life. It was here in her own community. Once the foreign white woman had gone, Yombe had to live among her own people. She could not risk being banished from the village. It was the only thing she had. She took a deep breath and headed back to her hut and her father's polluted corpse. As his only daughter, she had one last duty to perform.

Two weeks later, Heather paused before boarding the aeroplane at Kinshasa Airport. For a moment, she wondered whether she might be infected. It was highly unlikely. If she had picked up the disease directly from Yombe Embale's father, she would have been showing symptoms by now. She had informed the authorities about the death – just in case there was to be an outbreak – and then dreamed of going home to hot showers, clean water, books and music, civilization. She climbed the steps wearily. She was also thinking of Yombe. That poor girl. Heather wondered if Yombe was well, if she had made the right choice. Heather wondered if, out of sight of Ngoi and before she purged her father's body of its waste and undigested food, Yombe had slipped on the double-layer latex gloves and surgical cotton gown that Heather had left in the hut. These were the only protection that Heather could offer.

The midwife settled into her aircraft seat, scratched her itchy scalp and closed her eyes. She was relieved to be leaving behind those awful symptoms of illness. She hoped and prayed that she would never have to witness them again. She comforted herself with the fact that towns in England were not prone to that sort of disease.

Once the passengers had vacated the plane at Heathrow, an army of workers moved in before the next batch of travellers were ushered on to the busy aircraft. One group of technicians removed the sewage tank. Really, the ammonium salts added to the tank should have killed all of the germs in the passengers' urine and faeces but it was common knowledge that several infectious organisms could survive exposure to the disinfectant. The workers took no chances. They wore full protective gear. As usual, they took the tank to the airport outlet and they pumped the contents into the public sewer system. There, the waste from the tank was diluted and treated like all other sewage. The outflow would be chlorinated to kill the germs that typically turned up in British sewage. Once cleaned up, the effluent would be discharged into the river. Some was destined to become drinking water.

* * *

When, eventually, Heather reached her musty home close to Milton Keynes General Hospital, she forced herself not to flop immediately into an armchair and succumb to its comfort. Despite her exhaustion, she opened a few windows to let in some fresh air, made herself a mug of tea – the like of which she hadn't tasted for months – and unpacked as she sipped the wonderful, reassuring hot drink. When she extracted a pair of jeans from her suitcase and shook out the creases, she was surprised to see three – or maybe four – live flies emerge. Cocooned within her clothes, the flies must have escaped the pesticide applied to the baggage of the international flight. At first they seemed dazed and plummeted towards the carpet but they soon recovered and, buzzing healthily, made for the strong sunlight at the open window. In a few seconds, they had flown away into the alien British environment.

Chapter 2

Thanks to the animal rights lobbies, Laurie was not enjoying a drink in the university bar with her research students. Dressed as always in her white lab coat, she groaned as she waited at the goods entrance. It was yet another breathless night, not just warm but virtually tropical, after yet another sizzling day. Laurie wiped away the sweat from her forehead.

Two of the university security guards waved their arms theatrically and importantly like airport ground staff guiding an aeroplane to the right spot. The truck driver reversed his vehicle up to the back of the science block with hardly a glance at the men who thought that they were being helpful. The van's brake lights lit up Laurie's face and lab coat with an eerie red glow. For a second, she looked like an impatient and hungry vampire. The driver killed the engine, unlocked the tailgate, and stood to one side while, under the cover of darkness, Dr Henman supervised the discreet removal of the crates from the back of the truck. She took the first box herself and led the porters towards the animal house. She ignored the nervous scrabbling and scratching from inside the crate.

Outside in the back of the van, when a technician moved one particular crate he saw two loose mice. They had escaped from one of the boxes by gnawing around a knot in the wood and creating for themselves a small hole. The white mice scampered across the floor of the truck and dived out into the night like desperate convicts escaping from a prison. In the darkness, they soon disappeared. Only the technician noticed the breakout and he said nothing – in case he was blamed for their release. Besides, he thought to himself, the animals had been bred in such cushioned captivity that they wouldn't last long in the wild. Suddenly and nervously, he glanced upwards into the sky because he thought that he saw something – an unsettling black shape – and heard a strange fluttering. But if there had been anything above his head, it had gone. Perhaps, he told himself, a bird or bat was already on the trail of the scurrying mice. Soon, they would fall prey to an alert nocturnal predator.

Four security guards stood at each corner of the lorry. Two more stood at the end of the drive. They were all alert as if they were protecting a huge sum of money from imminent attack by vicious thieves. In fact they were there in case news of the delivery had reached the local animal liberation group. The anti-vivisectionists had already stormed the university biology department once and wrecked the labs of the pharmaceutical company across the road. Everyone had become ultra-cautious, sensitive and secretive about using laboratory animals.

The driver watched the circus as the university volunteers continued to empty his load of mice and monkeys. He was getting used to the precautions taken by veterinary centres, the pharmaceutical industry and universities that needed animals for their scientific research. He was used to the threatening letters and abusive phone calls from activists. He was used to checking underneath his lorry for suspicious packages before he set off on a delivery. He guessed that his Milton Keynes customer, Dr Laurie Henman, who was also gazing at the night-time proceedings with a wistful expression on her tired face, regretted having to get used to the same aggravation.

UNDERGRADUATE NOTES: MODULE 4; INTRODUCTION (i). L. HENMAN.
Unseen germs (bacteria and viruses) have fashioned human history. A human being may weigh sixty thousand million times more than a bacterium but the bacterium can kill the human being. A virus is even smaller (up to six billion of them can pollute a single drop of blood) and they are just as deadly. Tiny in stature, but major players on the world stage. The collapse of the eastern Roman Empire in the seventh century: bubonic plague. The defeat of Napoleon: typhus. The conquest of the New World: smallpox, flu, cholera, mumps and measles. Columbus carried smallpox to the Americas and, over the years, it has killed hundreds of millions of people there. In the

fourteenth century, one third of all Europeans were wiped out by bubonic plague: twenty-four million people dead because of an invisible warrior far more deadly than swords. In the winter of 1918-19, swine flu (Spanish flu) made half the world's population ill and caused more than twenty million deaths in six months. During World War I, human beings managed to slaughter only nine million soldiers and, even with all those weapons, it took four years.

Not all bacteria are bad for human beings. People are colonized by millions of bacteria that help to keep the less desirable ones away. Some aid digestion. There are more bacteria in the mouth of one human being than the total number of people that have ever lived on the planet. In many ways, humans are bacteria factories. There are more bacteria cells in a person than there are human cells. One sneeze will propel a million bacteria into the air in a force eight gale of a hundred thousand droplets of mucus.

Viruses are not alive but they are capable of life when they invade living cells. A ten millionth of an inch across, a virus is a package of genetic material wrapped in a jacket of protein, sometimes with a greasy overcoat, sometimes sugar-coated. Inside a cell, a virus pirates the host's chemical machinery and churns out more copies of itself. That is its sole and single-minded purpose: to reproduce itself as many times as possible. Viruses do not eat, grow or have sex; they just multiply. They travel inside carriers like insects, rats, mice, dogs, fowl, bats, pigs and monkeys. Typically, people become infected with a virus by coming into contact with the animals' urine or droppings, or through an insect bite. Then the disease spreads from person to person through infected droplets from the lungs (sneezing, coughing) or by direct contact with infected blood or body fluids.

Chapter 3

"Oh, Megan. He's done something all over the carpet! Ugh! Do you know how much we paid for it? Pure wool. It wasn't cheap, you know."

Megan snapped at her husband, "Don't be such a bore, Barry. No need to make a big thing of it." She was much more concerned about the well-being of their new pet than a bit of wool that he had fouled. Besides, it wasn't as if they were Tinkers Bridge people. They weren't poor. They could afford to replace the whole carpet – the very best – if the dog had ruined it. Or they could pay for a carpet cleaner to come in and do their dirty work for them. Megan was convinced that on the neighbouring Tinkers Bridge estate such a

19

mess would not get cleared up properly at all. Disgusting.

Megan and Barry Revill, and their son, were lying on the plush carpet, gazing under an armchair where the dog had immediately installed itself. "You know, Mum, I still don't think it was a good idea to bring him back. It must be quite a culture shock for him. South America one moment, a front room in Milton Keynes the next."

Megan did not like dissent from her son. "Hardly the next moment, Justin!" she barked.

He shuddered. His parents were the only ones to call him Justin. After seventeen years, he should have got used to the ridiculous name that they had inflicted on him but it annoyed him more every time he heard it. All his friends called him Rev.

His mum continued to defend her dog. "He's been in quarantine for the last six months. Poor thing. That's what's upset him. He'll be fine once he remembers us and trusts us again. Barry, go and get that big juicy steak. That'll do the trick."

"Yes, dear."

At Christmas, the Revills had splashed some of their ample money on an exotic holiday. They had trekked across Peru, Bolivia and Brazil. Seeing all the sights, getting back to nature, as Barry had described it. But they'd only stopped in plush hotels and the four-wheel drive had got muddier than their walking boots. In Bolivia, the beagle puppy had latched on to them when they'd fed it. They had driven more than a hundred miles from its home, over the border and into Brazil, before they'd realized that the clever creature had secreted itself among their bags in the back of the jeep.

They should have dumped him before they'd reached the airport, of course. He would have scrounged on the streets of Rio like the shantytown kids. But, no, Megan had made a decision. And that was it. End of argument. Confusing the dog's dependence with affection, she'd decided to adopt and rescue him. It was her way of taking a stand against South American poverty. Some people would have given money to charity or directly to the destitute kids on the streets. But Megan Revill avoided the shantytowns like she avoided Tinkers Bridge and saved a hungry hound instead. That was her bit towards solving an international problem. Her decision confirmed Rev's long-held view that his mother was semi-detached from reality.

She'd decided to call the beagle Darwin because Charles Darwin – of evolution and survival-of-the-fittest fame – had sailed to South America on board a ship called the *Beagle*.

Megan spread out a copy of *The Times* on a patch of the lush carpet. She took the meat from her husband and placed it across a headline: MYSTERY BUG WIPES OUT AFRICAN VILLAGE. The cowering Darwin was tempted out into the open by the smell of a luscious meaty bribe. He was short, and mostly brown and white. Across his back there was a saddle of black. He slapped both paws protectively over his prize and tucked into a blood-red steak bigger and better than many human residents could afford.

Tired of watching his mum buy more friendship, Rev got to his feet. "Anyway," he announced, "I'm off out." His parents had reached the age when they seemed to belong to a different species – *Homo sapiens ridiculus adultus*. Or maybe they were aliens. Anyway, to Rev, they were a profound annoyance and embarrassment. They even wore slippers.

"Where are you going?" his dad asked.

"Bletchley sports hall. Squash or table tennis."

His mother's nose wrinkled. "It's a bit run down. Who are you going with?" she checked, clambering to her knees.

Suspiciously, Darwin stopped chewing and watched the movement around him.

"Scott," Rev fibbed.

"Scott," his mother repeated in a murmur, as if she was calculating the worthiness of her son's friend. She came to a judgement. "Scott's a nice boy."

The beagle scratched furiously at his underbelly of short dense white hair with his dumpy back leg. Barry looked down and grumbled, "I hope he hasn't picked up fleas in those kennels."

"They did look a bit low class," Megan pondered distastefully. "Not quite right. Perhaps we'll have the vet take a look at him." She turned to her husband and said, "Time you sorted out the mess. Let's make sure it's done properly. Call a carpet cleaner."

"Yes, dear."

Rev sighed and left, feeling that his movements had also been vetted and disinfected by his overbearing mother. Except that he wasn't going to do what he'd told her.

It was something about her face. Lucy's face was naturally tanned and her black hair fell in thick curls to her shoulders. She must have inherited some Mediterranean genes from someone in her family. Her glasses were small and round and brown-framed – so cheap that they could have been trend-settingly expensive. She had a fun-filled face, always smiling, always with a hint of mischief. When she grinned, her whole face crinkled warmly with self-satisfaction and her glasses moved up her nose. Sometimes she wore a hat that made her look like a sweet small child – until she smiled and became a little devil again.

It was something about her manner. When she walked her arms swung vigorously, purposefully. In each of her steps there was an energetic bounce – even though her trainers were not Nikes, Reeboks or Adidas. They came from the back of a cowboy lorry that sold all sorts of goods without labels when it was parked in the lay-by in the Tinkers Bridge estate. Lucy Metcalfe was short, pleasantly plump and attractive. When she talked to anyone, she'd put her hands on her hips and lean close as if she were whispering confidences or state secrets. Sometimes her words were uttered with such enthusiasm that they tumbled into one another and barely made sense.

And it was something about the way that she wore an old crop-top. It hung down from her large bust like an apron of snow overhanging a high ridge. In the chill-out dance, when Rev held her waist, he really touched *her*, not a handful of blouse. She felt smooth and soft. It made him tingle in a way he'd never tingled before.

Rev hung around outside Boots at Lucy's knocking-off time. He was tense. He didn't know how she was going to react. Yesterday, she'd stormed away from him, telling him where to get off. He was hoping that last night's quarrel was nothing more than a tiff that every couple had. What had it been about anyway? He couldn't really remember or understand. Perhaps it was because, whenever he held her, he always seemed to be trying to claim her and, when she touched him, she seemed to be just having fun. Perhaps it had been a row about possessiveness. If Rev's parents knew about Lucy, they wouldn't have approved. She was from the wrong estate. She didn't have the right background, family, money and connections. That's why Rev kept her under wraps. That's one reason he liked her so much. Parental disapproval added to her allure.

In the heatwave, the concrete of Bletchley shopping centre acted like oven walls. It was baking. Sweat dampened Rev's T-shirt.

When Lucy came out of the shop with a couple of mates who also worked the tills, she muttered, "You're here? Why?" She jutted out her chin in an expression of exasperation.

"To see you. I thought we could..."

"After last night, you've got a cheek, Rev." She turned to him and, under her breath, said, "I mean, I'm not some poor little girl to be owned by a boy with big money and a big sports car."

Rev believed that his parents had given him the car on his last birthday so he didn't have to mix with the people who used buses. He was certain they used it as a bribe when they pressured him into taking A-levels. Actually, he adored the car but he pretended not to.

"Sorry," he replied, head down. "I just. . ."

"I might see you at the club – in a day or two. Depends how I feel." She walked away with her friends. After a few steps, she looked back at him but she hardly slowed her pace.

For a few seconds, Rev watched a fly walking audaciously up his bare and freckled left arm. Then, when it started tickling unpleasantly, he brushed it away with a shirty flick of his right hand.

Later, Rev leaned on the bar casually, kept his underage voice as gruff as possible, and asked for two pints of beer. Rev's mate, Scott, kept out of the way in the garden at the back of the pub because he looked his age, or if anything even younger than his seventeen years.

Sitting down at the wooden picnic table and handing a pint to Scott, Rev said, "I know she's not everyone's idea of the perfect girlfriend but . . . I don't know . . . she's *real*."

Automatically, Scott Henman realized that Rev was talking about Lucy, his on-and-off girlfriend. With a smile, he replied, "Have you met anyone who isn't real?"

"Plenty. My mum and all her cronies – especially the ones with daughters who I'm supposed to go after. Anyone my mum calls respectable. Lucy's not like that. Down to earth. Real." He took a long drink and then asked, "Scott, how do you know when it's serious with a girl?"

"Easy. After you've gone out with her, if you're dying to tell your mates all the sordid details and you do, it's not. If you're dying to tell everyone all the sordid details and you don't, it's serious. Because you're breaking out in a rash of respect: respect for her. Keeping what you have private. That's when it's getting heavy."

Rev nodded slowly. "And how do I know if Lucy's serious about me?"

"You believe me when I say she is. She'd have walked out on you ages ago if she wasn't keen."

"So why does she dish me out such a lot of grief?"

"Because she's showing you who's boss, laying the ground rules. In her own sweet way, she's just told you she didn't like whatever you did last."

Cheering up, Rev said, "That's the thing with you, Scott. Not experienced, never get up to anything, but you're always on the ball.

Cool as a glacier. Even my mum rates you."

Scott shook his head. "Bad news."

"She's got a dog now. Darwin."

"I hope it's well behaved or it'll be in trouble."

Rev said, "Not yet. He's just arrived, so they're in a honeymoon period. It won't last long."

"Where did she get him?" asked Scott.

"Bolivia."

"Bolivia?"

"That Christmas break we had."

"Well, I hope they've checked him over for diseases," Scott commented.

"Oh, I don't know. Mum could do with a dose of something nasty."

As Scott watched a group of bare-legged girls walking towards the pub in the dusk, he waved away some irksome insects and said, "If this weather keeps up it'll be like Bolivia here. Rainforests in middle England." Even at night, the end of June this year was exceptionally warm and humid. "You know, my mum's never taken me anywhere but Scotland and France. Too busy. Scotland was full of gnats and the French trip was to get me through GCSE oral."

Rev's eyes followed Scott's, but he took no interest in the newcomers. Thinking of his South American trip, he said, "How come everything really nice is so far away?"

"It isn't," Scott replied. "Not really. It's just that we don't see it when it's all around us."

"You mean you can see it in Milton Keynes? Your eyesight must be getting iffy."

Chapter 4

UNDERGRADUATE NOTES: MODULE 4;
SPREADING OF VIRAL DISEASES (i).
L. HENMAN.
A steamy rainforest teems with viruses that cause no harm to their natural carriers: bats, monkeys, reptiles, etc. The microbes are harmless as long as they are left alone. Trouble flares up when human beings start clearing the forests, destroying the animals' habitat, sight-seeing, coming into contact with the viruses for the first time. The displaced animals might infest a village and infect the locals; tourists might be bitten or sample fruit that has been licked by infected fruit bats. The human immune system (its self-defence) is accustomed to dealing with common viruses

like colds but it will not be able to counteract a new virus in the same way and it cannot have been conditioned by vaccination against an unfamiliar disease.

An infected local would be taken to a hospital. Hospitals are perfect for a virus. They contain lots of sick people with damaged defences. Ideal fodder for spreading. The more crowded the hospital, the better for the virus because spreading is more efficient by close contact.

The tourist may travel on a plane and take the virus to another continent within hours – before symptoms appear. International travel is a joy to once isolated viruses. They are taken for free on a world tour. Mountains, oceans, impenetrable rainforests and sheer distance no longer isolate them. The barriers are coming down and the world is becoming a global village. That means all humans will share everything with each other – including disease.

Chapter 5

No one messed with Aaron Wishart. He was totally weird. A complete off-his-trolley nutter. No one knew what was wrong with him or why he was a good few molecules short of a normal metabolism. In fact, no one knew for sure that he *was* weird. But everyone said he must be. For one thing, he never left his posh house in Woughton Park. Everything was delivered. No one even knew what the recluse looked like. Rumour had him completely covered in warts, never cutting his fingernails, a murderer who had bricked up his wife in the cellar, a dwarf, a giant, bald with staring eyes, hair down to his ankles, a horror story writer. He lived on his own. Didn't have a car. Never answered the doorbell. If a football went into his garden, it was a one-way trip. His place was built like a fortress. Not even the people who delivered his stuff had seen him. They had to announce their arrival at the entry phone and, somewhere in the house, Aaron would unlock the electronically controlled door. They were under instructions to leave their shoes outside, place Mr Wishart's order in the porch and leave immediately. Totally weird.

Outwardly, Aaron Wishart was perfectly normal. Middle-aged, average weight and height, healthy, greying hair, rather pale, but he was a bit pernickety. Really, he was a lot pernickety – to the point of eccentricity. But he couldn't help it. It was just that he had a thing about coming into contact with germs. And, because other people carried germs, he had a thing about coming into contact with other people. Flimsy phone lines were his only attachment to society. He talked to people, worked, ordered goods and got news and information – all through the Internet.

Every time he went to the toilet, he followed a compulsive routine. First he dowsed the seat and handle with bleach. Then he washed his hands and used the toilet. Afterwards, he couldn't flush it straight away because his hands might be contaminated and he could not abide the thought of transferring the dirt to the handle, so he washed his hands again. Then he unwound two rounds of toilet paper because it might have been soiled by his fingers, dropped it into the bowl and flushed the toilet. He washed again. The procedure was still not over. There were the taps and sink to consider. He'd touched the taps with dirty hands so he washed the whole sink with strong disinfectant. Breathing a sigh of relief, he finished. But a few minutes later, he was utterly convinced that something was not right about the toilet. He became so anxious that he had to go back and check. Maybe he'd not flushed it after all. Maybe the flush hadn't been enough. Maybe a germ lurked somewhere. Maybe the tablet of disinfectant in the cistern needed changing. But the thought of lifting the lid filled him with fear. He imagined all sorts of microbes lingering inside. Just in case, he'd don gloves before taking a peek. If the blue block was getting small, he'd replace it or just add another – to be sure. Before binning the gloves, he raised the seat and checked that he *had* flushed the toilet and that the flush had done its job. Just in case, he'd pull the handle again. And, when the cistern had filled up, once more. Next, he had only to wash his hands again, to go over the seat, handle and cistern lid with more disinfectant, and the job was done.

Except that sometimes he felt the need to change and wash his clothes as well.

Terrified of catching a dangerous disease, terrified of contamination, Aaron would wash his hands over and over again. Before and after touching his food. After touching any delivered goods. After touching almost anything. He'd get up in the night and wash again or take another shower. Antibacterial soap saved his life. On a particularly manic day, he'd spend two or three hours scrubbing his hands. He got so disgusted with his dirty clothes that he'd change twice a day and wash each load two or three times to make sure they were ultra-clean. The sheets on his bed, changed every morning, got the same thorough treatment.

Aaron Wishart knew exactly what was going on. There was information on the Internet and a book called *The Boy Who*

Couldn't Stop Washing. Some people with the same problem washed for eight or more hours a day – until they dropped from exhaustion with raw and bloody hands. Aaron managed quite well in comparison. If he'd seen a doctor, he would have been diagnosed as having a condition called OCD: obsessive-compulsive disorder. A hyperactive prefontal cortex in his brain affected his judgement and a continually turned-on caudate nucleus in his basal ganglia made him think that something was wrong all the time. It said so on the Internet. He knew that his obsession did not make sense and sometimes he tried to resist it but then he became so overwhelmed with anxiety that he'd nearly break down. Resistance was wasted effort. A doctor would have given him Prozac or behaviour therapy. But Aaron did not get either. For one thing, he couldn't go to a doctor's surgery: it was full of sick people with horrible contagious diseases. Instead, OCD had wrecked any hope of a normal life. But at least he was safe from germs. His house was sterile.

Chapter 6

Out of the dark crevice they came, one after another, until they hung in the air over the canal like a huge fluttering black cloak. Then, as one, they moved out from under the bridge to begin their nightly hunt.

The grotesque creatures flew skilfully on membranous wings, twisting, turning, diving, negotiating the narrowest gaps faultlessly. Even in the gloom, they swooped expertly on flies, gnats and moths, snapping them up in mid-air. The colony formed a black cloud and moved over the canal and the fields at the edge of Tinkers Bridge, obliterating every airborne insect in its path. The forbidding cloud floated across the farm, twisting through the trees, and crossed the river that bound the university before hovering above the campus. There, the swarming predators gorged themselves on the insects that had been drawn to the lights left on in some of the empty buildings and the eerie lamps in the deserted lanes and walkways.

It was an ordinary day at Milton Keynes General Hospital. Wards trilled with insistent high-pitched bleeps as patients pushed buttons to call nurses. The bed-ridden inmates were like hungry young birds, unable to fly or fend for themselves, calling to their parents. Equipment was wheeled endlessly from nest to nest. Some of it was hi-tech with flashing LEDs. Most looked like giant mobile coat-hangers from which bags of clear liquids or blood were suspended and drip-fed into the worst cases. There was the sudden unearthly clatter of aspirator motors for the asthmatics, the thunder of an X-ray machine shoved into a bay in an emergency, the loud snores and wheezing and coughs of the very sick, nurses calling to one another across the corridor, someone throwing up violently and copiously and at very high volume. And there were notices stressing the need for peace and quiet.

Very occasionally, consultants would stride into the ward for a few minutes, scattering lesser beings before them like a car driven through a brood of chickens. A consultant's entourage, nurses bearing clip-boards and the patient, absorbed every precious word uttered by the oracle like children showered with gifts at Christmas time. These pronouncements became the law of the ward. Yet some commandments were impossible. The prescription of a liquid-only diet when there wasn't one on the menu, for instance. "Make that bowls of soup and tell the patient to manoeuvre around any bits of vegetable and croutons." The prescription of total rest and quiet for a patient who was a metre away from an asthma victim with a painful blood clot in his leg who swore at the top of his voice every half hour, used the chugging aspirator several times a day, and had a screaming baby granddaughter as a regular visitor.

Here, on the conveyer belt of cure and care, no part of the anatomy was special or private. Every bit was just another component of the human body that could be diseased and in need of treatment. The most personal parts were no different from fingers, arms or toes.

Reticence and sensitivity were out of place. "Let's take a look at it. Mmm. Sore, isn't it?" A little prod and a moan or a scream. "Mmm. Double the dose, nurse. We'll have it back in working order in no time. Don't you worry. Now, who's next?" The wards were a kind of limbo with two doors. All of the patients who were on the mend were desperate to leave by one door and get back into the real world. Those who knew they could not be cured were trying to come to terms with their next destination, wondering what was behind the other door.

But through it all there was a camaraderie in the face of the common enemy: disease.

The exception was the maternity ward. Sure, there was pain. But there was an equal amount of joy. "Nearly there," Heather said to the heavily pregnant Jessica, smiling reassuringly. "Won't be long now." She glanced up at Jessica's partner who was standing at her side, feeling useless. "Are you all right?" Heather asked him. "You're not going to faint, are you?" It was a close, steamy day and the air-conditioning had never worked properly.

Oliver laughed limply. "No. I got a sore

throat. And I'm knackered. Aches and pains, you know. It's all this." He nodded towards his horizontal wife. "Not sleeping well." He wiped his throbbing eyes.

"Well, in here, mum comes first, baby comes second, and dad's a poor third. If you drop, we'll ignore you till mum and baby are OK. And Jessica's got more on her plate right now than worrying about you."

Oliver said, "Sure."

Heather thought that Oliver's face and neck were flushed and swollen. "If you're not well, go and see your GP," she advised.

"It don't hurt too bad. Maybe after. . ." Again, he indicated his wife. He smiled awkwardly at her.

Drops of sweat showed on both Jessica's brow and Oliver's.

There was a cry from the adjacent delivery room and Heather excused herself. "Sounds like your neighbour's going to beat you to it," she said to Jessica from the doorway.

After the midwife left the room, Jessica turned her head towards Oliver. "If you want, you go. I. . ."

Oliver put up a palm stained with grime and

paint. "I promised I'd be here, didn't I, and here I am."

"As long as you're OK."

"No worries," Oliver fibbed.

His immune system was despatching every weapon at its disposal through the narrow crimson tunnels of his body to confront the surging viral armies. From his lymph nodes to his liver, white blood cells engaged in running battles with the rapidly growing hordes of the rampaging virus. Very soon, his defence would be outnumbered and outwitted. It had never seen such an enemy before and it had no way to combat the threat. It had never learned how to deal with such an invader. His throat was filling with lymphatic fluids. Unseen, blood had begun to seep into his lungs.

When it was Jessica's time, when she yelled her third obscenity and the baby's head appeared between her legs, Oliver's eyes were not focusing properly and his brain was muddled. Through the blur, he saw a hideous alien's head emerging from his wife, cruelly tearing her apart. He shook with a sudden chill, uttered a cry of horror and collapsed.

"There goes another," Heather muttered.

"It's a good job we don't rely on men to give birth."

When it was all over and Jessica's bloodied bundle of wrinkly skin and bone nestled against her chest, Heather bent down to examine Dad. For a moment, she froze. His bloodshot eyes reminded her of something she thought she'd left behind in Zaire. "My God," she whispered to herself. "Please, not here." Immediately, she dashed to the internal phone.

The consultant looked over his half-moon glasses and said to Heather, "I don't think there's any reason to panic. This man has all the symptoms of flu."

"But his eyes. . ."

"A bit bloodshot, certainly. I've seen flu do that before."

Heather was still concerned. "It's just that I saw something like this in Zaire and I'm worried in case I've brought it back."

Like an impatient father addressing an excitable and inexperienced youngster, the doctor said, "You're a midwife, aren't you?" The disdain was dosed carefully.

Heather nodded. She felt like an ugly

duckling in the presence of a beautiful swan.

"I'm keeping him in but, between you and me, it's not for the patient himself. I'd prefer to send him home. But I'm protecting his daughter. He shouldn't come into contact with the baby at this stage. Not till she's a bit stronger and hopefully Dad's past the infectious stage." Then, white coat flaring behind him, the consultant hurried away to his next appointment.

Heather didn't sleep that night. She thought of Yombe, Yombe's poor father, and blood. Rivers of blood.

The next day, the consultant had to swallow his pride. By the afternoon, it was obvious that some strange disease was ravaging Oliver Church's body. He had been vomiting blood. His eyes had become deep red. Blood was leaking from his nose and mouth. His eyes, gums and even his nipples were bleeding. The ward sister told the doctor that the patient's diarrhoea was also blood red. He was badly dehydrated.

"Right," the consultant said quietly so that the other patients could not hear. "There's a midwife called Heather something. I want to speak to her again. This isn't flu any more. I've never seen an inflammatory response like it but maybe she has. Get samples to chemical pathology. I suspect his liver and kidneys are blocked with coagulated blood and tissue. But now he's run out of clotting factors so his blood's thin enough to leak from just about everywhere. Keep him on a drip to maintain fluids and electrolytes. We've got to keep his vital organs functioning so he can fight the disease himself. I'll put him on antibiotics in case it's a bacterial infection. There's not much more we can do for him till we get those results. But let's shift him to Isolation. Just in case. Besides, his appearance will upset the other patients."

"And my nurses," the sister added.

Heather took one look at Oliver through the glass and the worst fears of her restless night had become reality. He had tremors, occasionally writhed in agony, and he had thrown back the sheets because contact with his red skin caused too much pain. "That's it," she confirmed dismally. "Exactly what I saw in Zaire. If it goes like it did there, he'll die in twenty-four hours, forty-eight at the outside."

The pain killers had helped Oliver a little but not a lot.

To a nurse, the consultant said, "OK, get his wife and her baby back in for observation. Different room. And let's ask her what he's been up to. Has he been out of the country, ill, taking anything? Who's he been in contact with?" Then he added, "No results on his blood yet, I suppose?" When the nurse shook her head, he said, "Tell pathology it's important. Highest priority. We could have a major incident on our hands if it's an infection and he's been contagious for a while. Get a message to Ward 19 where we put him first. I don't want any of their patients to be discharged until we're certain they haven't picked it up from him."

Before, Heather had not been sure. She was willing to be comforted by the consultant's diagnosis of flu. But now Oliver's condition was unmistakable. He could have been Yombe's father in Zaire. Immediately she volunteered herself for isolation and for tests. She was perfectly healthy but she was scared – not for her own well-being but because she could be a carrier of the disease. If it was contagious, she could have brought it from

Africa and unleashed it on England. But, if she was responsible, she knew that she would also be the key to stopping the infection in its tracks. Because she was not ill, her body must have repelled the disease. In her veins, there would be antibodies to the awful infection. She had to allow the chemical pathology unit to run tests on her blood and tissues.

The consultant nodded. "I'll get a nurse to take samples from you straight away. As far as isolation is concerned, though, it's impractical. You ought to stay on site till we've got it under control but we'll pack the Isolation Ward to overflowing if we're not careful. If it's an airborne infection like a cold, we'd have to isolate the nurses and patients of Ward 19, you, me, all my other patients and contacts, all your friends and those mums, dads and babies you've dealt with since getting back to England. It's not on. But while we're waiting for the tests to come through, make a list of everyone you've come into contact with, especially the new-born babies. They'll be the most vulnerable. If you really are the source of the disease, at least some of those infants will have caught it. Let's check."

Heather agreed. As the nurse's needle

punctured her skin and the barrel of the syringe filled with healthy blood, she also thought of the flies that had escaped from her luggage. With a feeling of utter horror and misery, she realized that the insects could be the carriers. She had brought them back and set them free. And she'd come back with headlice that she'd picked up in Zaire. They'd resisted the foul-smelling lice shampoo. Who had got close enough to her to be infested?

She worried most about all those babies she'd delivered. What sort of a world had she brought them into?

Oliver died before the results came in. A microscopic examination of his blood had not revealed any agents of disease. No parasites and no bacteria. Antibiotics that would have knocked out any bacteria had no effect whatsoever. Oliver had not fallen victim to a bacterium. When the microbiologists pumped his blood through the finest filters in the laboratory and then injected it into laboratory animals, the rats became very sick after one day. Plainly, the infectious agent in his blood was able to pass straight through the tiniest pores. Only one agent was small enough to do that. There was no doubt that Oliver had succumbed to a virus. An unknown one. The microbiology unit was still working on its identity.

The consultant groaned. "A virus. Infectious and much harder to treat than a parasite or bacteria." He shook his head. "Still, until there's a second victim, and a third, we don't necessarily have a major problem. Perhaps we'll get away with just the one."

He did not sound hopeful.

Chapter 7

The estates of Tinkers Bridge and Passmore were like two neighbouring but isolated villages, separated by a line of trees, a couple of playing fields, a lot of money, and lifestyle. People in Tinkers Bridge made things, people in Passmore made money. People in Tinkers Bridge lived on top of each other in long lines of poorly built, thin-walled, small terraced houses that opened directly on to the drab streets. People in Passmore owned detached houses of a fancy red brick, individual drives and garages, neat gardens front and back. On their well-spaced properties, they had ponds with fountains, swings and slides, elaborate bird tables, and parking space for several cars or a caravan. The two estates were adjacent but hardly aware of each other. The affluent could ignore the plight of the poor and the poor could decry the arrogance of the affluent without taking the trouble to get to know one another.

It was a day when Lucy *was* speaking to her wealthy boyfriend. Standing in the road of dilapidated cars, broken-down bikes, discarded toys, and recycling bins, Lucy cried, "That bloody dog! Look what he's done."

Holding Darwin's lead, Rev groaned. "Blame my mum."

"I don't think she did it," Lucy quipped. Firing on all cylinders, she said quickly, "I mean, Passmore folk are better trained than the rest of us. Or so they tell us."

"No," Rev replied with a grin. "Mum landed Darwin on us."

Lucy snorted, "He's even got an upper class name. Despite his toilet arrangements not being upper class."

Already several excited flies had gathered on the dog's excrement, drawn to it by the irresistibly enticing smell. Two local mongrels strolled up to have a sniff at the alien beagle and his little present from Passmore.

Malcolm Rose

Lucy grinned and said, "It don't do my street cred any good to be seen out here with *two* boffins."

"That's only Scott," Rev replied, jerking his thumb towards his friend. "Not me. I'm not clever enough."

"Oh, that's right. You're just loaded," Lucy teased him. "A snob. Got to do A-levels because Mummy and Daddy say it's the right thing to do."

Rev admitted it in good humour. At least Lucy was talking to him even if she was throwing insults. "But Scott's doing six A-levels," he said.

"No, I'm not," Scott retorted. "Just Biology, Physics and Maths."

"I meant you're doing my three as well. Helping me through them."

Without warning, Scott slapped his own neck. When Rev and Lucy looked at him with puzzled frowns, he explained, "Been bitten by something, I think." He rubbed at the place below his ear where he felt an immediate itch. "Hope it didn't walk all over Darwin's mess first. Yuck."

"You'll live," Rev replied with a laugh.

*   *   *

UNDERGRADUATE NOTES: MODULE 4; SPREADING OF VIRAL DISEASES (ii).
L. HENMAN.

Viruses pick on the weak. People at war, sick people and poor people are easy prey. Diseases like flu have always thrived in cramped urban squalor because it has all the right conditions for contagion: high density of victims for easy transmission; lots of insects or rodents – other potential carriers; poorly nourished and immunodeficient human beings.

Cells of the immune system (the ones that fight invading diseases like viruses) do not last long in the body. They die off even quicker if the person is not getting a varied diet. Without good nutrition, the body cannot make enough replacement cells so it cannot combat a virus. Then, almost any pathogenic microbe can cause fatal disease.

Therefore, cities and hospitals are microbial breeding grounds. They provide a wealth of opportunities that are not available to germs in rural settings where the population is more sparse so that microbes cannot be passed around so easily.

*　　　*　　　*

From an open window, there was a screech. "Lucy! Get your backside in here. You're wanted."

"Why?" Lucy yelled across the untidy street.

"Tammy Smith's mum wants you to go and see her. Tammy's not feeling well."

"OK. I'm on my way." With a sly smile, Lucy said to the boys, "Amazing how popular I became when I started working at Boots." She winked. "I mean, I'm supplying the whole of Tinkers Bridge with discount drugs."

Rev and Scott walked with her as far as Tammy's modest home. Before she banged on the Smiths' door, she agreed to see Rev at the club that night.

Lucy's neighbour was lying on the battered sofa, eyes shut and a quiet involuntary moan coming from her mouth. "What's up?" Lucy asked Tammy's mum.

Mrs Smith shrugged. "Started with a sore throat. Then aches and pains, she said. Something like flu."

"Funny time to get flu. I mean, the middle of summer. Has she been to the doctor?"

Mrs Smith laughed derisively. "Appointment in ten days. She'll be back on her feet by then."

The sixteen-year-old was still flat out on the couch, unaware of Lucy's visit.

"What do you want?" asked Lucy.

"Don't know. Can you get us something for flu tomorrow?"

Lucy nodded. "Sure. No problem. It looks like she needs it." Tammy wasn't a particular friend but Lucy was still concerned for her. Besides, the neighbourhood always pulled together in times of need. It was a community spirit born of living together in hardship.

But Tammy didn't need the medicine. She needed much more. When she next opened her eyes, her mother took fright. There was something very strange going on. Mrs Smith dashed along to a neighbour who had a phone and dialled 999.

The hospital was only a brief minute away by ambulance – just on the other side of Passmore. The motion seemed to upset Tammy. For her, the journey was one pro-tracted minute of dreadful pain.

Normally in Accident and Emergency it would take time to see a real consultant but the hospital found one remarkably quickly to examine Tammy. She seemed to get preferential treatment, leaping ahead of the broken bones, the sprains and splinters. Then, within minutes, she was whisked away to a special ward with a nurse called Heather Caldbeck. Mrs Smith was bewildered by the speed of developments. "What's going on?" she stammered. "What's wrong with my Tammy?"

The consultant looked at her with commiseration in his eyes. "We think your daughter's got a virus," he explained. "She's probably infectious so we're having to isolate her till we're sure what's going on."

Tammy's mother was lost for words.

"Now, we need you to stay here and answer a few questions. We need to know all about Tammy. Where do you live?"

"Tinkers Bridge," Mrs Smith answered on auto-pilot.

The consultant nodded. "Do you know Oliver Church? He lived in Tinkers Bridge as well. A sort of odd-job man."

"There's lots of odd-job men in Tinkers Bridge. No, I've never heard of him."

"Do you think Tammy would have come into contact with him?"

"I can't see why she would." Still in shock,

Mrs Smith mumbled, "What are you getting at?"

The doctor didn't answer. "I've got to go and help with your daughter now. A nurse will be along in a minute to ask you a few more questions."

"Is she going to be all right?"

Ominously, the consultant replied, "We'll do all we can for her."

Tammy's coloured eyes told the doctor everything. Standing by her bedside, he said to Heather, "That's it then." He shook his head. "Confirmation that we've got a serious problem. Time to call in the specialists." To a nurse, he said, "Get me the number of the Communicable Disease Surveillance Centre."

When Tammy turned her head restlessly, a lock of her hair fell out and stuck to the pillow. Heather did her best not to show her shattered emotions. It was bad enough to lose a brand new father. Now there was a girl no older than Yombe Embale. The virus was easily the most cruel, uncaring, selfish, deadly thing that she had encountered. Worse than any weapon. Weapons could be controlled, banned or dismantled.

The consultant looked at her significantly and asked, "Are you ready?"

Heather nodded.

"OK. Get on with it while I phone. I don't want any delay. Half a litre immediately. Once the virus really gets a grip, I doubt if anything will dislodge it." He left Heather to the nurses and his junior doctor.

Heather knew what was going to happen next. Her blood serum was going to be injected into Tammy. It was probably Tammy's only hope. If Heather was well because her blood contained an antibody to the virus – a tiny particle that could identify the virus, latch on to it and disable it – then she could share it with the girl. It would give Tammy the weapon she needed to fight the disease. If Heather's blood didn't have the secret ingredient, Tammy would be on her own. They could only make her as comfortable as possible, monitor her fluids, replace nutrients with a drip, and pray for her.

Willingly but nervously, Heather bared her arm.

Chapter 8

In the stifling heatwave, Darryl Wheeler arrived like a cool breeze. About thirty-five, in jeans and a T-shirt, he looked nothing like a doctor. The proud slogan emblazoned across his chest proclaimed: *Laboratory animals liberate humans*. The investigator from the Communicable Disease Surveillance Centre took one look at Tammy, who was not responding to Heather's blood serum, and dialled his chief on a mobile phone. "Darryl," he announced. In a voice that suggested ruthless efficiency in spite of amazement, he said, "It's a haemorrhagic fever. Strange as it may seem, right in the middle of England. I can spot it at twenty paces. No, absolutely no doubt. You want me to take over?" He listened carefully to the reply and then said, "You got it. Send me a full team and BL4 conversion facilities." A minute later, he said, "I can't tell yet. Once we've got some samples and a few more victims, I'll decide. Have the army on standby with all their gear and police back-up. I'll let you know the area as soon as poss." He put the phone away and to his bemused audience of the Regional Health Manager, a doctor, two nurses and Heather Caldbeck, he said: "Listen carefully. I'm in charge. If we don't bring this under control, if we don't contain the epidemic that's on its way, Milton Keynes is going to become one great big overcrowded graveyard."

Stunned, a nurse said, "You're calling in the army. Are we under curfew?"

Darryl nodded. "Better phone your nearest and dearest if you live outside Milton Keynes. It could be a while before you get home."

Looking the younger man up and down, the smartly dressed Regional Health Manager questioned, "By whose authority?"

Darryl did not have much time or sympathy for administrators. "Check your rule book," he replied. "CDSC. Grade 1 outbreak. You're out of your depth."

"But. . ."

"Just ask your consultants if they want responsibility for this." He pointed to the dreadful sight of a bloodied Tammy on the other side of the window. "Or if they want me to step into the firing line instead." Darryl didn't wait for a response. He began to rattle off his first set of instructions like a confident teacher who had just brought a class under control. Tammy was to be placed in a negative-pressure plastic isolator. All of the hospital's patients without viral symptoms were to be sent to other units as soon as beds could be arranged – in case the whole hospital had to be dedicated to the infection. There would be no further admissions except for the infected. That way, they'd restrict in-house spreading because there'd be fewer potential victims for the virus to inhabit. All staff were to be kept on the hospital site or in the immediate vicinity. Family and friends of victims were to be kept in if they showed the slightest hint of symptoms. If not, they were to be sent away and placed under home quarantine.

When he'd finished, there was silence until the Regional Health Manager said, "We've only got two victims. Isn't this all a bit extreme? A bit drastic?"

Chillingly, Darryl asked, "How many deaths do you want before you admit you're at war? Two'll do for me. Besides, there'll be more."

In the large conference room, surrounded by his CDSC colleagues and unfamiliar hospital staff, Darryl began, "Before we start this briefing, let's not forget we've got one young woman who's going through hell right now. How is she?"

Heather Caldbeck answered desolately, "Temperature 107. Painful red skin rashes, vomiting blood. I'd say she's got less than twenty-four hours."

Darryl drew in a breath. "It's not the way any of us would choose to go. Never mind a sixteen-year-old." He hesitated for a moment. When he continued, his expression displayed determination. "It's now our job to keep the numbers as low as possible. And to make sure we're safe ourselves. That's not selfish. Right now, we're the most important people in Milton Keynes. Keep that in mind. I don't want any of you putting yourselves at risk. Because that puts everyone else at risk." He paused again and then added, "If any of you doubt the threat, let me read a couple of bits from Oliver Church's autopsy." He waved the pages at them and said, "I've got lots here. It'd be quicker to tell you what was right with him. But try these. 'Wherever there should have been clear cerebrospinal fluid, there was deep red blood.' 'Spleen, kidneys and liver blocked with protein and dead cells.' 'Lymph nodes completely empty of white blood cells. Every last one must have been used ineffectually to challenge the disease.' 'His brain was soaked in blood.' Need I go on? We're up against a brute that turns human innards into a viral stew. According to these notes, Jessica Church said her husband first complained of aches and pains a couple of days before he started bleeding, which you remember was straight after she gave birth. Then it was forty-eight hours to the inevitable. We don't know the incubation period – from infection to the first signs of disease – but let's guess it could be about a week. If that's right, this virus does in about ten days what HIV takes ten years to do."

Darryl's silence was very articulate. After a few moments, he continued, "OK. Point made

– and taken, I think. Let's get down to business. Heather offered us a ray of hope but her serum isn't working on Tammy Smith. Why not? Three possible conclusions. The virus is the same as the one she met in Zaire, she's a carrier, immune, but her antibodies didn't work because the virus had already got too strong a hold on Tammy. Second, maybe it's the Zaire virus but Heather isn't the carrier. She wasn't infected so she hasn't got antibodies, so she's no help to Tammy. Thirdly – a daunting thought – it's a different haemorrhagic fever altogether. There are plenty to choose from. So where do we start to look for the source of our virus if it's not from Zaire? I'll contact the CDC – the Centre for Disease Control – in the States to get access to their banks of viruses and antibodies. They might be able to help us. They've certainly got the best data on exotic haemorrhagic fevers.

"At the moment we've got one big clue. Both Oliver Church and Tammy Smith caught it so there's got to be a connection between them. I understand they both live on the same estate. That's a start. Let's follow it up. Did they come into close contact? Once we know the link, we'll be in a much better position to find the source." He assigned two of his CDSC experts to the detective work. "We're lucky our virus isn't airborne. If it was passed around in the air, several people – like Jessica Church – would have breathed it in and gone down with it by now. Anyone could've got it by sharing a bus with Oliver Church. We know how it *doesn't* move around but we need to know how it *does*. That's urgent. I know of haemorrhagic fevers carried by rodents, animals and insects. In many cases, we haven't got a clue about the source. A couple of these viruses definitely come from contact with mouse or monkey urine and then spread between people by blood-to-blood contact. Some might well be transmitted through saliva, tears or urine." Darryl leaned forward on the table and emphasized, "Remember this. No part of our unprotected bodies should touch patients' fluids or suspected patients' fluids. All of us in this room are potential patients so, no matter how you feel about each other, no kissing."

There was not one giggle. Everyone knew that he wasn't joking.

The CDSC entomologist chipped in, "I heard some flies hitched a lift from Africa in

Heather's bag. That's one possibility. I'll also organize a collection of insects in the area, especially from this Tinkers Bridge place. Live moths, flies, cockroaches, headlice, bedbugs, spiders, anything. We need to test the lot."

"And all pets," Darryl put in. "We need blood and urine samples from them. Dogs, cats, rabbits, mice, hamsters. Whatever the residents've got, we need their fluids. And wild animals. If it moves, we want it. Rats, squirrels, foxes, birds. Are there any bats around here?"

No one answered. Most shrugged.

"Well, someone'll have to find out. How about an animal sanctuary or farm?"

"There's a farm just across the canal. Between Tinkers Bridge and the university."

Darryl nodded. "Samples from cows, sheep, chickens, then. And their fleas. Everything on the farm." He hesitated and then added, "Talking of the university, I guess they've got a Biology Department. Let's hope it's got an electron microscope we can commandeer. And an expert on disease or a microbiologist who can help. Has it got laboratory animals? If so, where did they come from? If there's monkeys, my money's on them. Blood samples from monkeys go to the top of the list. Bats come second. I'll pay a visit to the university and look into it."

Heather suggested, "I think we ought to trace everyone on my flight from Zaire to Heathrow. It'd put my mind at rest to find out if they're all still OK."

"Good point. Let's do it. Have you got any news on the babies you've delivered since you got back?"

With considerable relief, Heather reported, "All thriving. Obviously I didn't expose them. Thank God."

Darryl talked at length about the microbiological testing for the virus, the extra laboratory equipment he was bringing in to cope with the virulent samples, the search for the identity of the disease, for antibodies, for a cure. He didn't offer unrealistic hope, only the opportunity for hard, difficult and extremely dangerous work. "There are about five thousand known strains of virus," he stated as he gathered his papers and stood up, "and biologists have studied about five per cent of them. We've all got some work to do, I think. Let's not cock it up or we'll pay for it in lives."

Before he ushered everyone out to get on with their separate tasks, he said, "Finally, can the hospital or someone who lives nearby offer me a bed? Not that I'll see much of it."

It was Heather who responded. She was pleased that this biologist was making her feel valuable. When she'd volunteered to help, he had welcomed her on to his team immediately without questioning her training. "My place is just over the road in Peartree Bridge and I've got a spare room," Heather said. "You're welcome to it."

"It's a deal. Thanks." His appreciative gaze lingered on her just a fraction too long.

In the university's animal house, Darryl walked among the cages thoughtfully. Monkeys uttered loud piercing shrieks and swung from rung to rung. Some just sat sadly and quietly in captivity. White mice, some shaven so that they looked like wrinkled bags of bones, cowered in plastic containers, nibbled food, slept or scrambled around, sniffing the air constantly as if expecting something awful to happen.

Darryl Wheeler had already explained to Laurie Henman why he wanted to see her urgently. "So," he said, "all the mice are genetically engineered to suffer diabetes?"

"I use them to test out potential cures for diabetics," Laurie replied. Thinking about this charismatic man's earnest words about the outbreak of a hideous infection and the need to find its origin, she added, "They've never been out in the real world so I can't see how they could pick up a virus – or any other disease apart from diabetes. Quite the opposite. They're the most mollycoddled creatures on the planet."

"But the monkeys?"

Dr Henman exhaled. "A research batch of African green monkeys from Uganda. They arrived just the other day. They're used for my research on vaccines. I've never had problems with my source before. All monitored and licensed. But I'll get blood samples to you straight away," she offered.

"Thanks. Any monkeys or mice escaped?"

Laurie shook her head. "No."

"Not even within the building?"

"Not to my knowledge. I'll check with my research students but they should've reported any incidents."

"Your field is medicinal – finding cures and preventing disease."

"You make me sound like a cure-all, Professor Wheeler," Laurie responded.

Darryl put up his hands and winced. "Darryl, please."

When he'd first telephoned, Laurie had looked him up on the Internet. Obviously a very bright kiddie. He'd published lots of papers on infectious diseases, studied with the best groups in America, witnessed the dreaded Ebola virus in Africa, become Britain's youngest Professor of Biology. Bright *and* fearless.

"OK. Anyway, I wish I was a cure-all," Laurie continued. "But I've only got three research students. It's a small group looking at a few specific projects."

He replied, "But you've got an electron microscope and you know all about microbes."

Laurie smiled wrily. "I teach it as a topic. Bacteria and viruses. That doesn't make me an expert. I'm not in your league."

"Laurie, right now in MK, you're a very important person. Will you help me?"

"I'd like to but I don't have the facilities to handle anything as virulent as what you talked about. My lab's only cleared for Level 2 biohazards. Something like Ebola scares me silly."

"Good. I don't want bravado. And I'll get your lab modified and upgraded to Biolevel 4. Just like that. My paymasters will cough up. No expense spared." He grinned and added, "I bet you've never had such a tempting offer without filling in an infinite number of application forms for funding."

Laurie laughed. "That's true." She was struck by the man's simple and direct attitude, his informal air of authority, and by his conviction. For a man who had to get things done, he was friendly and affable. "Yes," she said. "I'll do anything I can."

Chapter 9

UNDERGRADUATE NOTES: MODULE 4; INTRODUCTION TO INFECTION.
L. HENMAN.

A plague is coming. In May 1993, a new strain of hantavirus killed within hours almost every one of the Navajo tribe in New Mexico who contracted it. The disease is carried by a common rodent in the USA. In 1976, the Ebola virus swept through fifty villages in Zaire, killing 325 of its 358 victims. The natural carrier of the infection was not proved but was likely to have been bats. In 1967 the Marburg virus got into Germany via monkeys, imported from Uganda. All of the human victims had handled the imported monkeys or their tissue samples. It is clear that viruses can jump from various animals to humans. When a species encounters a new virus for the first time, the virus is uncommonly deadly because the immune system is inexperienced. Frequently, by the time that an individual's immune system can counteract the newcomer, it is too late. The original animal reservoir for Marburg was never found. It killed many of the monkeys in transit so they could not be the true carriers. They were also victims.

There are many viruses, bacteria and parasites that threaten to overwhelm and annihilate human beings: HIV, encephalitic and arthritic viruses, flesh-eating bacteria, haemorrhagic fevers, Legionella, toxic shock syndrome, E. Coli 157, etc., etc. They are extremely nasty, frequently deadly, very difficult to combat, and often drug-resistant.

Chapter 10

Rev swallowed. His girlfriend was wearing this short spray-on dress that showed every contour, wrinkle, crease. He did not know whether to be excited, embarrassed, proud, or resentful of the attention she would attract. He decided to try to be excited.

As she strolled towards the hospital with Rev and Scott, Lucy said, "No, she's not a big mate, Tammy. Just someone who lives down the road. I'm going to visit her because us Tinkers Bridge folk stick together. That's all."

Lucy seemed to know everyone on her estate and everyone seemed to know her. Rev was ashamed that he didn't even know the names of the people living opposite his own house in Passmore.

"Tammy sits around all the time grumbling about how fat she is," Lucy recalled. "But she hardly eats anything. I mean, if she sees some lads laughing, she always thinks they're laughing at her. But she's much thinner than me. You boys wouldn't understand. I've thought about going on a diet a million times but I've never done it. I'm too lazy or don't have the willpower."

"Don't you dare go on a diet," Rev replied. "You're fine. I don't want you to disappear."

"No danger of that." She slapped her thighs and commented, "I mean, more Teletubby than supermodel."

"Perfect."

Lucy was remarkably open and honest about things. "I guess I'll just carry on squeezing myself into a size 12. That way, I don't feel fat, even if it's a bit stretched. Better than admitting to being a size 14."

The three of them came to a sudden halt. A bulky policeman was blocking the walkway near the hospital. Much to Rev's disgust, the cop's eyes covered every millimetre of Lucy's body as they approached. To make a point, Rev took her hand in his. "What's up?" Lucy said to the police officer.

"Hospital's closed."

"Don't be daft. You can't close a hospital like it was a shop," Lucy snapped. "I mean, have people stopped getting ill?"

"It's only open for certain emergencies," he explained without really explaining.

"Well, we're visiting someone in emergency," Lucy replied, refusing to be intimidated by this cold official.

"Who?" the policeman enquired.

"Tammy Smith."

"Are you relatives?"

"Friends," Lucy claimed. She uncoupled her hand from Rev's and adjusted her hat to keep the blinding sun out of her eyes.

"Just a minute."

The police officer backed away and deliberately spoke into his radio so the three youngsters could not hear. Then he said, "OK. I'll find out and tell them." Coming up to Lucy, the cop said, "Were you close?"

Lucy frowned. "Were? Not especially close, no. But close enough to visit her and wish her well."

To their left in the car park, they saw a scuffle like a rugby scrum with shouts and squeals.

"The press," the policeman said abruptly.

"What's going on?" Lucy said, her face creased with concern. Suddenly, she feared for Tammy.

Softening his voice, the policeman said, "I'm afraid. . ."

She didn't hear much more. She didn't need to hear it all. Something about an infectious virus. Something about keeping away. Something about Tammy dying.

It was a hot airless night. Lucy, Rev and Scott sat despondently outside The Moorings alongside the marina and watched the moths and dragonflies congregating around the outside lamp. Occasionally, Scott rubbed the sore lump on his neck where the gnat had bitten him.

In a hushed voice, Rev said, "These days I only think of a virus as something that gets inside a computer and screws it up."

Scott explained, "Computer freaks nicked the word from biologists."

Lucy sighed. "Why didn't they just zap Tammy's bug with drugs?"

"You'd have to ask my mum for a proper answer," Scott replied, "but antibiotics don't work with viruses. They only zap bacteria."

"Viruses, bacteria. All the same to me. And to Tammy. She's still dead." Lucy put her head in her hands.

Rev placed a sympathetic arm round her shoulders.

Scott told them, "Mum said she'd seen this chap from the hospital about a virus yesterday. He called on her at work. She's agreed to do some research on it or something. I didn't know it was anything to do with your Tammy." He shook his head. After at least a minute of silence, he said, "Tonight I feel like doing something . . . a bit crazy. What do you think?"

"Like what?" Rev said.

"Something that I'll be ashamed of if I get caught – or proud of if I don't."

"Like?"

"Like taking all my clothes off and jumping in the canal."

"Boring. Matt did that last year after GCSE exams. Hurt himself on a submerged Tesco trolley."

All three of them looked up. A strange dark silhouette hovered overhead. Several black shapes plunged out of the sky like empty crisp packets caught in a downward draught. Lucy covered her hair with her hands. "Bats!" she cried. They headed for the moths and dragon-flies, picked them off in an instant and were gone.

Rev looked into Lucy's normally cheerful face only for a moment before his resistance crumbled. He wanted to comfort her. But he wasn't sure how. He gave in to his instincts, leaned forward and kissed her. Lightly at first and then more passionately.

UNDERGRADUATE NOTES: MODULE 4; INTRODUCTION (ii). L. HENMAN.
The skin around the mouth is home to many microbes and the mouth teems with different bacteria. In between, the lips are less populated with live organisms so when people kiss lightly on the mouth only a few microbes move between the participants. A little more passion and the outer layers of bacteria are ripped away from their moorings on the teeth. Grease from the corners of the mouth is torn away, along with spurts of acne bacteria. A passionate kiss generates a wind tunnel effect, a howling gale for bacteria and viruses, which stream from one person to the other with the sloshing saliva. In the fervour of a

kiss, the male's body temperature and hormone levels increase, intensifying the female's desire. After, if the kissing couple rest their foreheads together, the invisible families of demodex mites living on their eyelashes interchange, hunting for food like mascara or acne cream.

Rev rested his forehead on Lucy's. Suddenly, though, Lucy pulled back from him, adjusted the glasses on her nose and said, "This isn't right. I mean, not after Tammy. . ." She rose and backed away.

When Rev stood up and volunteered to walk her home, Lucy said, "No. It's all right. It's just. . ." She paused and put out her hand. "OK."

Refusing to play gooseberry, Scott said goodbye to his friends and watched them stroll along the towpath in the direction of Tinkers Bridge. Once they had disappeared into the humid night, Scott did not feel like analysing his strange mood. But the reason for it came into his head anyway. He'd been affected by the death of a girl he didn't even know. He wanted to make a mark on the world because, like her, like anyone, he might not be on it for long. Tomorrow he could be run over, crash down the stairs on to his head, catch a virus. Suddenly it made sense to live for the moment.

For a while, he thought about going into the pub, adding a year to his real age, and ordering a few drinks. But he decided against it. Once, he'd wanted to be the hard guy who could binge on beer, but he didn't like drinking too much alcohol. He didn't like the taste or the hangover. And the thought of being out of control on drugs turned him off completely. He didn't really know how to be reckless.

He could go inside The Moorings, see if there was a girl and, for once, find the courage to chat her up. But he never knew what to say. Besides, he admitted to himself that no girl would think of him as a prize catch. He wasn't good-looking like Rev and he was small for his age. He was frightened of rejection.

Yet he couldn't just go home and get on with some schoolwork. That wasn't exactly racy. Doing homework wasn't going to secure his place in the history of the planet. Anyway, he'd seen for himself that there was no link between academic effort and reward in life.

His mum was clever – very clever – but she worked long hours for a salary that barely covered the living expenses of their Passmore house. How did all the rich people get rich? Because they're incredibly hard-working and incredibly intelligent? Scott thought of Rev's mother and father. They got rich because Mrs Revill inherited a pot of gold and Mr Revill dealt on the stock market for a few years before retiring early with a huge packet. Smart perhaps, but not intelligent. Barry Revill had made nothing apart from money for himself. He hadn't cured a cancer, or even made a car, cooker or computer. He'd contributed nothing to the community.

Scott didn't want to be ordinary. He hoped to strike out and make a difference. He wanted his footprints on the Earth to remain long after he'd died. But how?

He sauntered along the towpath on the Woughton Park side, skirting round the overgrown bushes that separated the houses from the canal. The unruly brambles and branches threatened to push him into the still, black water. If Tinkers Bridge had houses, then Passmore had mansions and Woughton Park had palaces. Scott occasionally caught sight of an expansive and expensive garden and brightly-lit house through the hedge. In one place, the owner had built a great big fence around his property. It poked out from the top of the bushes. The house was rumoured to be a mad recluse's bolt-hole. Four Tinkers Bridge lads were scrambling over the hedge to spray obscene graffiti on the fence. A bit of a waste of time, Scott thought, if the owner was a hermit. He wouldn't come out and get the benefit of the boys' literary style and artwork.

Two of the lads confronted Scott. "What are you looking at?" they barked.

"Nothing," he murmured rather pathetically.

The other two turned round. By the moonlight, one of them recognized him. "Hey. You're one of the two Passmore jerks that hang out with our Lucy."

Another drawled, "Are you both having her?"

Scott sighed and looked away.

"You're not thinking of sneaking off and telling the cops about this, are you?" The boy inclined his head towards the embellished fence.

Scott answered, "No." The amateur painters and decorators were younger than him –

probably fifteen or sixteen – but he was clearly outnumbered.

One of them suddenly turned the aerosol on Scott and sprayed the front of his shirt with bright red paint. "No, you won't. They'd look at that," he said, pointing to the stain, "and you'd get done for being a vandal."

The others laughed. The one that laughed the loudest roared, "Steamin'!" Then, suddenly changing mood, he bent his head down, gripped his nose between forefinger and thumb, and groaned.

The lad's distress made the others laugh even louder. "Second nosebleed tonight, Tony! Good going. One day you'll pee blood."

"If you're going with Lucy," the leader said to Scott, "you must fancy yourself as one of us." He was standing in front of Scott, blocking his path.

Scott hated the tribe mentality but he didn't want to start an argument. It wasn't worth the risk of being beaten up or taking a dunking. "Lucy's a friend. No more than that," he replied lamely.

"A friend," two of them repeated in high mocking voices. "You mean she hasn't let you," they sniggered. "She lets everyone else!"

Scott could make a little mark on the world by defending Lucy. She wasn't like that, he was sure. These lads were just being lads. But he didn't defend her because he suspected that he'd be making marks on the towpath, by the time they'd finished with him. He tried to walk away but the one who had sprayed him with paint grabbed his arm. "If you're one of us, come on."

"What you got in mind, Gary?" asked one of the others.

Gary shouted back, "You'll see."

They scrambled through a gap in the hedge into the Woughton Park estate. Gary went first and the others pushed Scott through. "What's your name?" Gary demanded to know.

"Scott."

Tony, still nursing his nose, held Scott's left arm and another boy his right. When Scott looked down, he could see by the yellow street-lamps that he was a mess. The front of his shirt glistened. His left arm and sleeve were soiled with Tony's blood. The gang walked into the quiet road and Gary ambled around, his head down, gazing intently at the kerb, tarmac and verges. "What you looking for, Gary?"

"Something." He smirked and added, "Something for Scott. To show he's one of us." Eventually, he shouted gleefully, "Over here!" When his two mates had dragged Scott towards him, he pointed at the ground and said, "What's that?"

Scott grimaced. "Something that came out the wrong end of a dog."

"Ooh, very posh way of putting it," Tony cried.

Scott began to sweat. Gary's idea was going to be thoroughly obnoxious.

"You're going to pick it up," Gary said slowly, "and post it in Weirdo Wishart's letter-box."

"Good 'un," the others chimed.

"Steamin' idea," Tony said enthusiastically.

"It nearly *is* steaming!" Gary said with a wicked grin. "Go on, pick it up, Scott. Get your hands dirty for once."

Tony and his mate pushed on Scott's shoulders, forcing him to crouch down towards the kerb. "Pick it up," they ordered.

Scott shook his head. It was more an expression of disgust than a refusal. He imagined that he'd be in for something far worse if he didn't do what they said. He reached out. His palm hovered over the horrible moist pile, scattering the engorged flies, but the message to clench his fingers and grasp the stuff seemed to take an age to get from his brain to his unwilling hand.

"Go on!" the boys shouted in unison.

Scott swallowed and took a deep breath.

Across the road, a man with a big alsatian appeared at a door and shouted, "What's going on out there? Clear off!"

The pressure on Scott's shoulders suddenly lifted. He fell back on to the kerb. The four youngsters ran off laughing and swearing at the man. Relieved, Scott stretched slowly till he was upright again.

"And you!" the man yelled at Scott. "Or you'll feel what it's like to have my dog's teeth in your backside."

Scott did not hang around to protest his innocence. He did not try to defend himself by declaring himself to be a victim. Instead of thanking the good neighbour for his timely intervention, Scott dashed back to the gap in the hedge and clambered through it, on to the towpath. He looked down at his hands. Still clean. Even so, he wiped them against each other as if he could erase the memory of what he had almost been forced to do. Then, relaxing a little, he scratched at his neck and resumed his route home alongside the canal.

Dr Henman was rightly proud. She had risen from a tiny rundown terrace in Watford to a nice property in Passmore. OK, it was sometimes a struggle, but she'd made it. Many people in Milton Keynes would regard her salary as a fortune. She wanted Scott to enjoy things that she could only dream about when she was his age. She wanted him to think of life as fun, not a constant battle to afford bread and butter. She'd made it academically as well. She recognized that she wasn't going to win a Nobel Prize, but she was respected in her own field. Once, her parents had tried to persuade her that success was being a good housewife but instead she'd become a Doctor of Biology.

She looked up from her journal and her greeting froze on her lips. She stared at her son's chest, pointed and exclaimed, "What's. . .?" She jumped out of her chair and the journal went flying to the floor. Her breath came in short gasps as she went into an uncontrollable panic.

Scott reached out, touched her arm and said, "It's paint, Mum. That's all. It's OK. Just an accident with some red paint."

Laurie hesitated and then flopped back into the chair. "I thought for a minute, you'd. . ." She sighed. "I thought it was blood." She recalled everything Darryl Wheeler had told her about haemorrhagic fever and the dreadful bleeding. For a few seconds she thought that Scott had succumbed to the virus. And that had petrified her. She was so unnerved that she forgot to query Scott's accident with the paint.

Instead, Scott asked her what she knew about Tammy Smith.

Straight away, his mum leapt in with a question. "You haven't had any contact with her, have you? Touched her?"

Scott had only ever seen his mum in such a state of anxiety once before. It was years ago when his dad had walked out on them. He reassured her by saying, "No. Not even close." He paused before adding, "Hadn't you better tell me what's on your mind?"

Laurie raised a weak smile. She had never

refused to talk openly to her son and she wasn't going to clam up now, just because the subject was unsavoury. In fact, she was relieved to have a listener. She could unburden herself and Scott needed to know the details to protect himself as much as possible. "Go get changed, make yourself a coffee or whatever, then we'll talk."

Chapter 11

Nothing. Absolutely nothing. Two days after Tammy Smith's death and no other victims had come in. Some of the hospital staff were wondering if all the fuss was for nothing. They were hoping it was for nothing. This pushy character from CDSC had come crashing into their hospital, created havoc, turned the place upside down, scared everybody, for two deaths. Sure, any two deaths were regrettable but they'd not be noticeable in the hospital's statistics.

Darryl was satisfied that the microbiology units at the hospital and the university had been upgraded to state-of-the-art maximum-security high-containment laboratories. Absolutely no organisms got in or out of these Biolevel 4 labs unless they were authorized human beings. And those humans would be the cleanest people on Earth. In one of the air locks, they would strip naked and take an unpleasant seven-minute power-shower with disinfectant detergent before dressing in head-to-toe protective suits. Two more air locks were lined with harsh ultraviolet lights that killed all microbes. On the way out of the facility, each scientist would have to go through it again in reverse order. They would emerge as pure and immaculate as angels. Their clothing would be incinerated. Before being vented, the air from the laboratory would be cleansed by microscopic filters, ultraviolet lights, a high-temperature oven to burn all organic matter, and several corrosive chemical scrubbers. All that Darryl needed now was a breakthrough. And he needed more samples. That meant more victims.

In the most daunting moment of his short stay in Milton Keynes, he'd also inspected the hospital's incinerator. He'd requested some changes before he was satisfied that the unit was capable of doing the grim yet vital job that he had in mind.

It was midnight. The waiting was nerve-racking. Life had become a vacuum, like the lull before the hurricane began its unearthly scream. Heather threw aside the two local newspapers with huge headlines: WHO'S NEXT? and PLAGUE IN MK. Her third rum and Coke in her hand, she said, "Don't get me wrong, but I'm interested. What qualifies you to do this job?" The alcohol had made her bold and talkative.

Darryl was sitting on her sofa with a cold beer. He thought about it for a second and then replied, "A bit of knowledge about biology and a lot of heart."

"I heard it was more than a bit."

With a wave of his hand, Darryl dismissed the notion that his scholarship was especially important. "It's compassion that counts. But before we get to the end of this, someone'll accuse me of being a hard-hearted bully because of what I'm going to have to do to beat it."

"Not me," Heather said quietly and sincerely.

Darryl looked into her face. "No, not you. Because, in Zaire, you found out what it feels like to be utterly helpless against a tiny but towering enemy that shows no mercy."

Heather ran a hand through her short hair. Her scalp was still itchy. "You could be somewhere exotic studying . . . I don't know . . . the life cycle of the blue whale."

Darryl laughed. "Size isn't everything. A blue whale weighs forty thousand billion billion times more than a virus yet, given half a chance, a virus will kill a whale."

"But that's the point. Studying whales is safe. Fighting viruses is likely to get you killed sooner or later."

"Perhaps. But so might driving up and down the M1." He took another soothing drink and said, "At least if a virus gets me, I'll have done some good first. And I'll have worked on the most fascinating things in the universe." Flippantly, he added, "Besides, someone's got to do it and I don't see a queue of eager biologists waiting to take over from me."

It was two-thirty a.m. when the call came in. The police had arrested a man making a nuisance of himself in Tinkers Bridge. Staggering, yelling, groaning in the middle of the night. But he wasn't a drunk. His eyes were too bloodshot to be merely a side-effect of alcohol. The hurricane had begun to howl.

Together Darryl and Heather sped to work in the dead of the night.

Even in the early hours, Darryl Wheeler's hastily prepared unit was buzzing. During the night, three victims of the virus arrived. At the hospital entrance, a large notice written in thick felt-tip read:

DURING THE PRESENT EPIDEMIC, THIS HOSPITAL IS CLOSED TO ALL OTHER PATIENTS.
RESTRICTED VISITING UNTIL FURTHER NOTICE.

The routine casualties of late-night accidents, alcohol and affrays were sent to Northampton, Buckingham or Aylesbury. The three un-mistakable victims were taken straight into Isolation. A seventeen-year-old girl and one man from Tinkers Bridge, and a young boy from Woughton-on-the-Green. The young woman was an acquaintance of Tammy Smith and, when she was admitted, the rims of her glasses and her plump cheeks were already stained ominously with blood.

"No bedside visitors," Darryl ordered.

"But what about relatives?" a nurse queried. "They'll go spare."

"Get an internal phone installed – so they can speak to their loved ones. That's the best we can do. If they're close enough to see them, they'll see things they don't want to see. If they're close enough to touch, they're close enough to get the virus and spread it around."

"But they won't understand. They'll still want. . . Mums and Dads'll want to be with their sick kids, even if it's not pleasant, even if they catch something."

Darryl replied, "I know. But it's our job to look after the sick *and* protect the well. Until we get more research done, we can't do much for the sick so our main priority's got to be protecting the not-yet-sick. They won't thank us for it but that's what we're going to do. Keep them apart. At least till we're sure how this virus jumps from one person to the next, how it puts itself about. But you can bet your life the patients' blood is infectious. We already know it infects lab rats. It'll infect humans as well. So, no contact – or you *will* be betting lives." He paused before continuing, "There'll be a problem with bodies as well. When they die, the relatives'll want them. No chance. They'll be teeming with infection. We'll keep tissue and blood samples, and the rest will have to be incinerated immediately and very thoroughly."

Darryl's finger followed the outline of Tinkers Bridge on the wall map. In his other hand he held a mobile phone. "It's time. Yes. Bring them in. Milton Keynes is carved conveniently into chunks by a grid system of roads. The hospital's a potential source of the epidemic, of course. It's part of Eaglestone. That's got to be inside the cordon. To the east, there's Peartree Bridge and Woughton-on-the-Green: one victim. South, there's a chunk containing Passmore, Tinkers Bridge, Woughton Park and the university. All the other victims live in Tinkers Bridge and I've got a helper at the university. Put the ring round them as well. If we include Netherfield to the west of Tinkers Bridge – in case the virus crosses the main road – we've got a nice neat square of four adjacent chunks. That's it as far as I can see so far. Relatively easy to contain. Blockade the main roads round those estates and stop the walkways – they're separate from the roads here – and it's sealed in. Unless it flies, of course. But the disease is so localized, we can probably rule out long-distant fliers like birds as the source. Besides, we can't stop them coming and going. We can rule out the river for the same reason: it would've carried the virus all over the place by now. So, let's get down to the nitty gritty. They've got coded roads in Milton Keynes: H for horizontal or east-west roads and V for vertical, north-south roads." He looked closely at the map and stated, "I'll rely on the army and police to seal everything – and I mean everything – in the grid bounded by H9 Groveway, V7, H7 and V10. The guards'll have to be armed to take care of any wildlife that breaks through. Rabbits, rats and the like. If you get a move on, the barricades can be in place by dawn. Simple."

Once the news had got around, there was chaos. The switchboards at the hospital and at Eaglestone Health Centre, attached to the hospital, were jammed. Every little twinge of pain was reported as if it were agony. A wince became a last gasp. It was hypochondriacs' heaven. A few of the calls were important, most were trivial, some were hoaxes. The trick was to distinguish one kind from the others, to bring in the serious cases and reject the time-wasters.

"My boy's not feeling well. I don't know what's wrong but he's grizzly. Won't sleep."

"I hate to trouble you when. . . It was in the papers, wasn't it? But I think I'd still better . . . just in case. You see, I've got this. . . Well, it's an ache. All over, really. And I'm worried in case . . . you know. What do you advise? Should I see . . . do you think?"

"I don't care if you are busy. I've been waiting on this line for ages. And I feel bloody awful. Serious, like. My arms and legs feel like lead bloody weights."

"I can't bring her in because she's disabled and I ain't got a car. Besides, with the runs like hers, she's not gonna make it without . . . you know what I'm saying? . . . without an accident. A messy accident."

Local people who thought that they might be infected were let through the cordon and into Accident and Emergency. A huge impatient queue developed in the waiting-room. Every available doctor helped to sift potential viral cases. Patients complaining of genuine flu-like symptoms were sent to wards that had been set aside for observation.

Emergency medical staff were brought in, experienced doctors on holiday were recalled, all leave was cancelled.

It was nearly sunrise and the procession of bats followed the course of the canal to Groveway. One by one they filtered under the road bridge and up into their secret lair. It was a cool cavity in which to rest and roost during daylight hours. They had learned to ignore the heavy harmless rumbling of the traffic on the road overhead. This time, though, there were unaccustomed noises as people on the bridge disgorged razor wire from the backs of huge camouflaged lorries. The sinister mammals were uneasy but they had to return to their home. They hung in the dark and conserved energy by turning down their body temperature, metabolic rate and heartbeat. Their heart rate dropped to a miserly four beats a minute. A controlled sort of hypo-thermia. They needed relaxation because their nocturnal flight and search for food had consumed vast amounts of energy. Their hearts had been beating one thousand times a minute, fuelled by a ravenous appetite for insects. That night, each bat had devoured more than two thousand insects – half its own body weight.

The returning colony was restless because of the unusual noises above. With an occasional flutter, they folded their tired membranous wings, gripped their perches with their feet and dangled upside down to recuperate.

After the events of the previous night, Scott felt weary and sluggish in the morning. Yet the anxious tone of his mother on the telephone downstairs forced him out of bed. She'd hung up by the time he slumped in front of his breakfast bowl. Behind him, she put both her hands on his shoulders and said, "Feeling all right?"

"Sure. Just tired."

"You may not see a lot of me over the next few days."

Scott twisted round. "It's started, then?"

"Sounds like we're back to the dark ages," she answered. "Plague in Milton Keynes, of all places." She sighed. "Apparently, we're surrounded by troops. The hospital, Netherfield,

Tinkers Bridge and Woughton. No one out, no one in."

"But. . ." Scott was thinking of all the things he wanted to do outside the restricted area. Looking at his empty bowl, he asked, "What about food? What about getting a new pair of jeans? There's a film I want to see in town as well. And there's the little matter of school."

"The army'll bring in food and essentials. That's it. As far as school's concerned, you've got an extended summer holiday, but an enterprising A-level student would get his work from school through the Internet." Briefly, Laurie perched next to her son. "It'll take some getting used to but hopefully it's not for long. Now, if I'm going to do my bit to beat this thing, I've got to get into work. You look after yourself, OK?"

"OK. You go. I'll be fine." As his mum was leaving, he shouted to her, "Give it some aggro, Mum."

"If I can find its ass, I'll kick it."

Chapter 12

Laurie and the CDSC entomologist could not help laughing. In the foyer to the Biology Department, there was a noisy group of parents and young children carrying match-boxes, jars and margarine tubs, punctured to provide air to the insects and garden pests inside. "Yuck. That's gross!" "I know you can't see them but they're there. Mum picked them out this morning. They're headlice." "My slug's longer than yours." "Well, I've got four flies and a frog. Except there's only two now. I think the frog got hungry." "My spider's not moving. I think it's dead. Do they check its pulse?"

Laurie called for quiet and then thanked them all for helping in the research effort. "We're going to take your names and a note of where you got your insects and things. Then we've got to try out a few tests on them."

One young girl piped up, "Are you going to kill them all?"

Aware that she might offend the sensitive children but unwilling to lie to them, she began, "Sometimes we've got to put the good of people like you before. . ."

The girl interrupted, saying, "Oh, good. You are. Can we come and watch?"

Scott dived into Rev's house, saying, "Have you heard? This plague thing. . . Oh, hello, Mrs Revill. Mr Revill. And hello, Darwin." The dog licked Scott's hand in greeting.

Straight away, Megan Revill stopped wiping the surface of the table with a damp reusable cloth and queried, "Plague?" Unbeknown to her, bacteria had multiplied on the kitchen cloth from its first day of use. Now it seethed with a billion invisible germs. Wiping the dirty table seemed hygienic but it distributed the bacteria. After Megan had finished, the table top looked cleaner but it was covered in unseen writhing microbes.

"Yes." Scott sat down and told them everything that he knew about the infection.

Immediately, Megan was indignant. "That's terrible! You mean we've been shut in with Tinkers Bridge? People will think we're part of the same estate."

Rev was very worried about Lucy. He decided it was time to rebel. "We *are*," he said abruptly to his mother. "We're the same postcode."

"Stop that before you start, Justin," his mother cried.

"What?"

"You know."

Rev said, "How can I stop something before I start?"

"You know I'm not talking about postcodes," Megan exploded. "I'm talking about . . . something else."

"What's that?"

"Class."

"We're all the same class," Rev pointed out. "All human. All just as yummy to a virus."

Megan shook her head in despair. "Then tell me why this wretched disease is only affecting them, not us. Obviously, they brought it in."

Scott tried to end the discord. "Mum said it's probably just because they live closer together so it gets passed from person to person more easily. That's all. And she said someone from Woughton-on-the-Green's got it."

Megan turned her head away in disbelief. The fact didn't fit her theory about class so she ignored it. Instead, she banned Rev from going anywhere near that awful, disease-ridden Tinkers Bridge. "Filthy place."

Rev took a deep breath and said, "What are you going to do, Mum, when the virus gets its first Passmore victim? Kid yourself it's not happening? Claim that Tinkers Bridge polluted us nice people?"

She replied, "I wouldn't put it past them to do exactly that."

Rev shook his head in annoyance and stood up. "Let's go and look at the barricade," he said to Scott.

His mum added, "Take Darwin for his walk while you're at it."

Scott knew what was on Rev's mind. Yes, Rev was curious to see what the army had done but first, as an antidote to his mother, he wanted to call on Lucy. He needed to make sure that she was all right – especially because she'd been in close contact with Tammy Smith.

It was Mrs Metcalfe who answered the door. She looked worried. "Who are you?" she barked at the two young men on the pavement outside her shoddy house.

"Just friends of Lucy. We wondered if she's around."

Suspicious, Mrs Metcalfe mumbled, "Funny sort of friends." She told them, "Lucy was supposed to go to work this morning but she couldn't make it."

Rev's face crumpled with dread. "What's wrong with her?" he uttered.

"It's not her. Seems soldiers are stopping everyone leaving."

Rev let out a long breath of relief. "Can I speak to her?" he said.

"Stay there," Mrs Metcalfe ordered.

From behind the half-closed door, Rev and Scott heard her boom, "Lucy! Boys here for you."

While they waited, Rev said to Scott, "Phew. For a moment there, I thought she'd . . . you know."

"Caught it?"

Rev nodded.

Lucy came out, in shorts and a top that seemed to have shrunk in the wash, put her hands on her hips and said, "What's going on? Do you two know? It's a prison camp round here, like being back at school."

"What happened?" Rev asked her.

"I went to get a bus into town as normal. But there was nothing doing. I mean, no cars, no buses. The road's blocked from Groveway. The Simpson roundabout's covered in barbed wire and soldiers. Some've got guns," she said irritably.

"Let's go take a look," Rev suggested eagerly. He perked up once he'd realized that Lucy was unharmed and in her usual fighting spirit. "Scott'll fill you in on the way."

"OK." She shouted to her mum that she was going out for a while and closed the door before she got a reply. "I'm really annoyed," she announced. "We was going to have a fun competition at work today."

"Competition?"

"Yeah. When you're on the tills, customers lean towards you and breathe all over you." She illustrated on Rev. "We was going to score them all – slight onions to vindaloo via three-star nasty niff – and see who'd got the smelliest breath." She laughed and added, "Don't worry, Rev, you wouldn't win."

Scott put in, "A lot of bad breath's down to bacteria chomping through food left on the teeth."

Frowning, Lucy realized that Scott was getting round to the subject of disease. "Is that what this soldier thing's all about? Something about Tammy's bacteria or virus? Some stupid idea to stop it getting out?"

"That's what Mum said." Scott told her everything else he'd learned from his mother.

Groveway underpass, the route that all the little kids used to get to the middle school, was completely boarded up. The pupils would be overjoyed. The first pieces of graffiti had already joined the official *No Entry* sign attached to the wood. Above, at the side of H9, there was barbed wire and the head of a soldier bobbing past. Scott, Rev and Lucy walked along the path between the ends of the terraces and the road till they came to the bus stop on V8. Eerily, there was no traffic but to their left Simpson roundabout was a mess. More razor wire blocked off the dual carriageway that ran between Tinkers Bridge and Netherfield. The tangle of steel ran alongside Groveway in both directions like a perverse, impenetrable and thorny hedge.

Beyond it, and beyond the soldiers on sentry, police officers were directing the chaos of traffic, reporters were stampeding towards any bewildered residents who appeared at the barrier, a fire engine was standing by, cars and vans with Central TV and BBC logos were parked in Marlborough Street. There was a jumble of thrusting microphones and cameras.

A voice from among the jostling journalists shouted at them, "What do you think about being treated like caged animals?" Another yelled, "Have any of your friends been infected?"

Speechless, Rev put his arm round Lucy's waist and Scott stood with a hand over his brow to cut out the dazzling sunshine. They did not have the slightest intention of answering the questions. They were struck dumb by shock. Abruptly, the place had acquired an oppressive, ghetto atmosphere. They were the tainted, the unclean, not fit to move among the unaffected. They had been separated and forcibly cut off. Suddenly, they were dangerous creatures to be guarded, quarantined in a ring of razor wire, patrolled by the army to prevent escape. It was an awful feeling. Rev experienced shame as if he personally was threatening to contaminate the world. Lucy felt defiant. She wanted to rush at the wire, tear it down and berate her captors. Scott accepted his imprisonment as necessary. He wished that he could play a part in beating the disease. *That'*s how he could make his name. Whoever cracked the virus would be a hero for ever more. But it couldn't be him. He was just an A-level student.

After a stunned minute, Scott, Lucy and Rev turned away like exhibits in a zoo, tired of the gawping.

Every house in Woughton, Tinkers Bridge, Netherfield and Eaglestone received a circular. It explained the circumstances of the quarantine, apologized for the inconvenience, and called for calm, restraint, co-operation and patience while the authorities went about their task of ending the scare as quickly as possible. The confined residents were all invited to a meeting that night at the university where a Professor Darryl Wheeler would explain their predicament in detail and answer their questions.

*   *   *

Gathering the team together in the conference room at the hospital, Darryl called for strong hot coffee, health bulletins and helpful results.

"Right," he uttered, bringing the meeting to order. "We've got two sorts of people: the infected and the healthy. So, we need two solutions. A cure for the infected and a way of stopping the thing spreading to the healthy. If we can only come up with one solution, it's got to be some way of stopping new infections. Prevention's better than a cure. Without a cure, we'd lose everyone who gets the disease but we'd make sure no one else gets it. Keep it tight. That's much better than having a cure but no way of preventing the disease. It's no good letting everyone get the virus and then dragging them back from death's door with drugs. Hospitals won't cope and lots of people would slip through the net and wouldn't get treated anyway – even if we could make enough of some wonder-drug. It's too awful to think about. So, priority one is containment. Where's the virus hiding? How does it infect its victims? How does one victim pass it to another? That's what we need to know." He took a drink. "Someone tell me there's a neat connection between Tammy Smith and Oliver Church."

"Sorry. Only one link," one of his CDSC investigators replied. "Living in Tinkers Bridge."

"That's it?" Darryl queried. "There's got to be something more. Did you check out Church's odd jobs? Any bring him into contact with Tammy Smith?"

"He didn't exactly keep full records. Proper records of jobs complicated his tax return. But the Smiths didn't have any work done on their property. A quick glance at it told us that anyway. Tammy had a Saturday job at an animal centre. And, no, they didn't have any jobs done by Church either."

"An animal centre." Darryl was keen to learn more. "What did she do there? Any exotic animals from Africa or wherever?"

"She was used as a manual worker, helping out in general. She cleaned up after the animals and that sort of thing. We got our animal handlers to take blood samples from every animal they had on site. No overseas ones. Of course, Tammy would've contacted plenty more that were brought in for treatment, inoculations and so on, and sent home straight away."

"Are you tracing them?" Darryl asked.

"Working on it. But Oliver Church didn't have a pet. There's no obvious link between him and Tammy's animal centre."

"Look for ones that aren't obvious, then. Were any of the animals from Tinkers Bridge?" Darryl enquired.

"They treated a pet cat with a broken leg. It came off worse in a collision with a car. We've given the microbiologists a blood sample from it already."

"The car wasn't driven by Church, was it?"

"Bit of a tragedy, that. The cat's owner ran it over."

Darryl turned to his microbiological team. "What's happening with all these samples? Any joy yet?"

"Both Oliver Church's and Tammy Smith's blood infects rats. They start dying twenty-four hours after they've been injected with it. That's the test for the virus. None of the other blood or urine samples – household pets, wild animals and Dr Henman's lab animals – have the same effect on the rats. They're clean. So, no, we haven't found the source yet."

"Not even the monkeys?"

"They drew a blank."

"This flattened cat?"

"Administered. We're still waiting to see how the rats react to it. The other samples from the animal centre are in the queue to be tested."

"Mmm. A bit slow, isn't it?" Darryl remarked. "Twenty-four hours before we get results."

Laurie chipped in, "I'm trying to speed that up. I know Oliver Church's and Tammy Smith's blood is riddled with the virus so I'm using it to develop a faster test. And I'm trying to isolate the virus itself."

Darryl nodded appreciatively. "A fast test would make a world of difference while we're sifting samples to find what's carrying the virus. And if we could actually see what we're up against . . . great. Get an electron microscope picture of it and we get a psychological boost. We win the hide-and-seek game. Then we've just got to hammer it. We can start feeding it anti-viral drugs under the microscope and see if there's any reaction straight away. Keep it up, Laurie."

"Insects are still coming in, as well," she told him. "I don't know what they teach kids in schools these days. Since when are slugs and frogs insects? Anyway, if I can speed up the test, we can get to work on them."

One of Darryl's CDSC biologists reported, "I got a sighting of bats. A colony last seen outside a Peartree Bridge pub where they raided the insects around the lamps. I'm getting nets ready to try and catch a couple if they do it again tonight. And I've got a patrol out, looking for their roost."

"Good. Mammals like bats are the prime suspects. I want them in the identity parade."

"An airborne virus from Heather's definitely off the suspect list," another worker put in. "I tracked down almost everyone on her flight from Zaire. One heart attack, the rest fine. No sign of infection."

"I'm still waiting for data from the CDC in America," Darryl said. "They're checking all their known antibodies against it. That'll take time." He glanced at Laurie as he added, "They'd identify it quicker if they had an electron micro-scope image of it." Then he asked his medical staff, "What are our latest battle figures?"

Heather answered, "Two more patients – two more youngsters – went downhill in the observation wards this morning. We've shifted them to Isolation. Five alive – for the moment. None of them showing any sign of winning, I'm afraid."

"So they're not going to give us the antibodies we need. Soon we'll be reduced to praying for snow in mid-summer. Cold would kill the virus off." Emotionally, Darryl whacked the table with his right fist and the coffee mugs quaked. "Where's this thing's weak spot? Don't tell me it hasn't got one!"

After his team had dispersed, Darryl took his mobile phone. He had to make a very important and private call to his parents' house.

Chapter 13

A big woman in a yellow dress got up at the public meeting and shouted, "My mum's ninety. She's in Beanhill and she relies on me calling to get her meals. I've got to see her every day."

"Come up afterwards," Darryl replied. "Give us her name and address and we'll make sure Social Services sort her out," he promised. "She won't come to grief because you're stuck here."

A man called out, "You say there's two dead and five infected. That's not much of an epidemic. There's more casualties when a bad case of flu goes round but we don't get this sort of panic. Aren't you over-doing it with this siege?"

"With respect, you wouldn't say that if you saw a victim. This is an absolutely ruthless virus. It's in a league of its own and if it spreads, it'll make the worst flu known to man look like a mild summer cold." Darryl was at his most convincing and domineering when he stressed, "We've *got* to lock this one up." There was no arguing.

"You said all we could do was look after our hygiene, avoid wild animals and kill indoor insects. Isn't there something like a flu jab?"

Darryl was brutally honest. "We don't know what we're dealing with yet so we don't have a vaccine. Till we identify it or someone gets infected but becomes immune or we find a drug that attacks it, we're in the dark. I don't want to give you advice that's wrong. That might raise false hopes or even put you at greater risk. But you'll get better advice as soon as we can give it."

"Doesn't penicillin fix it?"

Really, Darryl had already given the answer in his talk when he explained the difference between bacteria and viruses but he showed no impatience as he answered the question. "Penicillin's an antibiotic. Antibiotics knock out bacteria. We're well off for those drugs. OK, they let us down sometimes but we've got a good few to try on any bacteria that come along. Our problem's a virus. There are very few drugs against viruses. Hardly any effective ones. That's why we've never cured viral infections like the common cold, flu and AIDS. On top of that viruses keep changing. They're a moving target. That makes drug treatment particularly difficult. We'll work on it, but don't hold your breath."

A hysterical voice shouted, "So how are you going to cure it?"

"Look," Darryl replied, "I'm being frank with you. Right now, we're not sure. It's hard to attack an enemy till you know where it is and exactly what it is. First, we've got to carry on with our research. Identify it, find out how it infects us, and then we'll be able to see how to attack it or at least stop it making more of us ill."

"With all these soldiers and stuff keeping us in, you're not thinking of wiping it out by dropping a bomb on us, are you?"

"No," Darryl answered with certainty. "It's the sort of thing that happens on telly but this is reality. I can guarantee we won't drop any bombs. I can't think of anything worse. It'd kill us humans and scatter the virus all over the place. No chance."

Once the people had left the hall, Darryl sighed, loudly clapped his hands together and said to his weary helpers, "OK. Back to work."

At the end of Mr Wishart's drive, Phil stopped and examined the bottom of his left shoe. Screwing up his face, he muttered to himself, "It's not my day." He wiped the shoe on the grass verge to get most of the mess off, then he strolled up the drive, tool-kit in his hand. Some days ago, his partner had fallen sick and left Phil with all the jobs to do. Now, the powers-that-be had closed off the area – apparently it was something to do with Oliver's sickness – separating him from the rest of that work. He was grateful for the call from Aaron Wishart and the fifty quid he'd earn by fixing the man's front door after someone had tried, but failed, to force an entry in the night.

Phil announced his arrival using the entry phone. Mr Wishart had no intention of coming to the door but he opened it electronically so that Phil could begin his work. It was likely that someone had used a screwdriver to try and prise open the door. But it was a solid construction. It had not given way. The wood around the lock was damaged and part of the frame was splintered. Both needed attention. The lock itself would have to be reseated. Phil got to work with his left foot in the porch and the right outside. Attracted by the lingering smell on Phil's shoe, several insects buzzed around him.

When he'd finished and announced through the entry phone that the job was done, a plain brown envelope came through the letter box in the inner door and slapped on to the floor of the porch. Phil bent down and took the package. Looking inside, he saw five brand new ten pound notes. His eyebrows rose. What a strange way to get paid. What a strange, invisible customer. But Phil wasn't complaining. Fifty quid was fifty quid. He pocketed the cash.

When he closed the repaired door, he trapped a few insects inside the porch.

One of the two young men under the bridge let out a stifled cry as bats fluttered out of their niche in the bridge. The other whispered, "Shush. Only bats." The men ducked down till the dark procession came to an end. Then they looked up and swore. "Police've even blocked off the canal!" A bundle of razor wire had been stretched across the surface of the water. On both sides of the canal, the towpath was barricaded and the footpaths into Simpson were a mass of barbed wire. Impossible to get through.

"I've never seen anything like it," Pete hissed. "All this, police, soldiers and fences for a couple of break-ins. It don't make sense. Crazy."

"Well, I ain't sleeping rough here," his brother said. "Not with all those bats flying about. We got to get out."

The two young burglars had been caught on the wrong side of the barrier. Last night, while they had raided two homes in Woughton Park and failed to get into a third, the army sealed off the area. They were imprisoned at the scene of their crimes. They had kept their heads down during daylight hours. Now it was dark again they had to get away. If they failed, the police would catch them sooner or later.

Pete scratched his stubbly cheek and looked down at the canal. The foul water was like cold, unappetizing soup. "That's the way," he announced.

"What d'you mean?"

"Bet there's no wire *under* the water."

"So?"

"That's our way out."

His brother looked horrified. "I ain't going in there," Jim protested. "No way I'm going to go underwater. You never know what those bats have done in it. Yuck."

"All right. You stay here, then. I'll visit you in the nick."

Jim shook his head and changed his mind. "Oh, all right. If we have to. But what are we going to do with the goods?" He nodded towards the haversack, full of cash, visa cards, computer games and a laptop computer.

"I'll go first. You throw it over the wire to me when I'm out on the other side. And make sure you're on target. Half of that stuff's no good if it gets wet."

Pete lowered himself slowly into the murky water. As he did so, flies and gnats scattered from the surface. The water came up to his chest as he waded and stumbled towards the razor wire. At one point, he let out a cry of pain as his foot found a submerged object and slipped off it, twisting his ankle. At the barrier he took a deep breath, closed his eyes tightly, screwed up his face, and sank out of view. A few bubbles broke the surface but otherwise he had disappeared.

In sympathy with his brother, Jim held his breath.

Ten seconds seemed a long time. But then Pete's head and shoulders reappeared on the Simpson side of the wire. He shook his head, ran his hands through his short hair, wiped his eyes and spat a couple of times. Then he made his way to the bank and clambered out on to the opposite towpath. Dripping on to the concrete, he called in a hushed voice, "All right, Jim. Sling it over."

Jim took the bag and was about to throw it when he hesitated. "When I chuck this, you ain't going to leave me here, are you?" His words sounded hollow, echoing under the bridge.

Pete sighed. "Just throw it. I'll wait for you."

Jim swung the bag twice and let go on the third one. In the weak orange glow from the lamps set into the bridge, the haversack sailed across the gap. Pete took a step sideways, held out his arms and caught it like a precious baby. "OK," he whispered. "Your turn."

Much more hesitant than his brother, Jim slid into the filthy stagnant water.

"Speed it up," Pete said, looking round warily. "It don't do the ducks any harm."

"I ain't no duck." Jim winced as his feet sank in unseen slime and something solid touched his left leg.

"Come on," Pete implored impatiently. "Get it over with."

At the barricade, Jim stopped, unwilling to go under. To delay the moment, he brushed aside a discarded plastic bottle, a punctured football and a dead fish that were floating in the canal.

"It only takes a few seconds," Pete assured him. "Hold your breath, push off, a couple of strokes underwater and it's done. We're out of here."

Grimacing, Jim mumbled, "Sure." He breathed heavily three times and then sealed his lips together and pinched his nose tightly. He sank down reluctantly like a ship capsizing slowly. Underwater, he didn't strike out firmly or strongly enough. He was hindered by insisting on holding his nose. And, in his eagerness to get out of the water, he came up too early. He was on the other side of the wire but he felt the razors slicing into his back and clamping on his shirt. He cried out, wiped the water from his face and thrashed about. "I'm stuck!" he yelled.

"Shush," his brother urged. "They'll hear."

In panic, Jim boomed, "Get me out of here."

Above their heads a voice shouted, "What's going on?" It was a soldier on the bridge.

Annoyed, Pete snarled at Jim, "I've had it with you. Always cocking it up." Clutching the haversack, Pete dashed down the path, determined to make a run for it. If he could get into Hanmer Road, he could lose the soldier in the twisty estate. He scampered along the track like a frightened rabbit.

Perched up high, the soldier raised his rifle to his shoulder. "Stop!" he yelled. "I have orders to shoot." He waited a second for a response. Nothing. The man kept on running. In a moment, he would be out of sight. The soldier had a split second to decide what to do. "Stop or I shoot," he barked.

Scott opened the window wider to try and ventilate his hot and airless bedroom. But the breeze barely had the strength to stir the curtains. As he took some deep breaths of the fresh air, a single shot sounded in the quiet of the night. With a grin, he said to himself, "There goes a rabbit making a run for it. Don't put that in a pie and eat it. It's one for the incinerator."

Really, he didn't feel like joking. He was trying to cheer himself up because he was uneasy. It was after midnight and his mum had not yet come home from work. Perhaps she wouldn't tonight. Perhaps she was too busy. The house seemed big, empty and eerie without her. Suddenly, it struck him that, for the good of everyone, she'd put herself in terrible danger. She was taking on the most deadly virus ever to emerge in Britain, a project that was beyond her usual expertise. He wished that she would return.

Outside, a cat or a dog or a fox knocked over the dustbin and Scott nearly jumped out of his skin.

Chapter 14

When the steel barriers went up, the vicar of St Mary's Church had been trapped on the outside of the exclusion zone. Putting aside his own fears, Ross McGavin begged the authorities to let him in. His parishioners needed him now more than ever.

Only two police officers lived in the enclosed area and the authorities decided that they weren't enough. Especially after the incident with the burglars. Six police volunteers were assembled. With the reinforcements, each of the four estates would have its own pair of police officers. Three counsellors had also been commandeered for work within the besieged sector.

At dawn, before the residents had come to

life, a crane swung a cage containing the vicar, the counsellors and the constables over the stockade and into the danger zone.

When Scott had shown an interest in science during his GCSEs, his mother had nurtured his talent by fixing him up with work experience in her unit at the university. He was familiar with the Biology Department and its staff. At mid-morning, with no sign of his mum coming home, Scott decided that it was time to go back to the university.

While he ambled along the footpath by the farm, he waved a hand occasionally in front of his face to disperse the inexhaustible and irritating flies. To his right, a dead tree looked like a barren pylon against the blue sky. On its stunted bare arms, a family of ugly crows had collected. They seemed to be waiting for something, like fidgety vultures sensing impending death. Much to Scott's discomfort, they all appeared to be watching him. He quickened his pace.

The laboratory was unrecognizable. There were doors and reinforced windows where there had been nothing before. Scott stood on one side of the thick glass plates and watched his mum on the other side. She was standing at a negative-pressure isolation box, her hands thrust into the giant gloves. In her left hand she held a terrified white mouse. She'd turned it over, exposing its soft furry belly. In her right hand she held a hypodermic syringe. Carefully, she directed the needle towards the mouse.

Scott guessed what was happening. She was injecting the laboratory animal with a sample of infected blood. One little slip, an unexpected squirm by the mouse and the sharp needle could contact her glove. It could easily puncture the protection and expose her to the virus at once. That would be a hell of a sting – an automatic death sentence. Scott took a deep breath.

It was like watching someone defuse an unstable bomb. Or maybe a crook holding a loaded gun to his mum's head. Scott was seventeen, supposed to be nearly adult and independent. But what would he do without her?

"Scott Henman. How're you doing?"

Scott was startled by the technician's sudden greeting. He gasped, realizing that he'd been holding his breath as his mother completed the injection. "Oh, all right, I suppose, Colin."

Colin nodded towards the activity in the Biolevel 4 lab and remarked, "Not one of God's better ideas." He paused and then said, "The virus, I mean, not your mum. She's a very brave woman. Wild horses wouldn't drag me in there."

Scott remembered Colin well. He was capable of talking endlessly.

"What do you reckon?" he asked Scott. "Is God sending a plague for our sins or is the virus an evolutionary tool, weeding out the weak?"

Scott shrugged. "It just is, isn't it? I haven't noticed it picking and choosing its victims. Strong or weak, good or bad, it doesn't seem to make any difference."

"Maybe *all* us humans have become weak and sinful," Colin declared. "Or do you subscribe to the theory that the Government's been up to some biological warfare and something's got out?"

Mercifully, Scott's mum turned and saw her son on the other side of the pane. She pointed towards the exit to indicate that she'd finished.

Colin said, "It'll take her twenty minutes to

go through decontamination. Why don't you wait in the foyer? I'll tell her you're there."

"OK."

Laurie's skin was a brighter pink than normal. The coloration was a reaction to the antiseptic soap and the thorough scrubbing of every part of her body, at least twice a day. Looking tired but pleased, she hurried towards Scott, saying, "Sorry. I didn't have time to phone. I had to work through the night."

"That's all right," Scott lied. "Was it worth it? Have you got anywhere?" Really, he didn't have to ask. Her face said it all.

"There's a long way to go, Scott," Laurie answered. "But, yes, I've helped a bit. I've probably developed a better test for the virus. Much quicker and pretty easy."

"Not good news for mice, though," Scott guessed.

"True. They're sacrificed, but bear in mind the stakes. I'm not using them to test a new lipstick here. This is absolutely necessary." She hesitated and then enquired, "Are *you* OK?"

Scott nodded. "What's next on the agenda?"

"Update the boss: Darryl Wheeler."

"Then?"

Laurie laughed. "You're like a nagging mother, you are, Scott. Trying to hint I should take a break."

"You hint at me often enough when I'm struggling."

"You win." She held up her raw hand and Scott slapped it. "Let me make this phone call then we'll go home for a while. Besides, I've got to wait three to four hours for developments with the batch of mice I've just done. That'll clinch it, one way or the other."

At home, Scott made the coffee and, when he handed the mug to his mother, he said, "Your Colin thinks the virus is a curse from God or something out of germ warfare."

Laurie smiled and shook her head. "He would. But it won't be either. It's just one form of life doing what comes naturally: reproducing. I doubt if Colin would accuse a cold of being a Government conspiracy or divine intervention. But our virus is just like a cold – only nastier. And, luckily, not so contagious." She took a sip of coffee and added, "You know, I'm not surprised by this outbreak. I'm more surprised we haven't had a plague before. Viruses and bacteria are out there somewhere. In rainforests and the like." She thought for a moment and then admitted, "I suppose it's a punishment in one sense. When we poke our noses into forests, cut them down, destroy habitats, animal carriers are going to get displaced. We're just asking to spread microbes around. If we left well alone, we wouldn't come into contact with them."

"It's nature's revenge, then?"

Laurie shrugged. "That's one way of looking at it."

"Not so far from God sending a plague against sinners," Scott remarked.

"Let's not get too melodramatic – or morbid – Scott. It's too virulent to last long."

"How do you mean?"

"Well," Laurie answered, "think about it from the virus's point of view. It doesn't care about its victims, only about its continued existence. The most successful viruses are passed between people easily without harming them too much – like the common cold. That way, the germ spreads quickly – just what it wants. You see," she explained, "if a bacterium or virus puts its victims out of circulation and then kills most of them quickly, there's not much opportunity for the germs to pass around.

There's no advantage to the microbe in that. Bad tactics. They'd prefer people to stay alive, on their feet and mixing freely, coughing and spluttering. The super-savage ones have never become big epidemics. They aren't so infectious. They pop up now and again but they're too successful at killing to last long. Ours is the same."

Scott asked, "What if one of the really deadly ones, like ours, suddenly learned how to become mega-infectious? Couldn't that happen? Maybe in the incubation period, before a victim knows they've got it."

Unwillingly, Laurie nodded. "A mutation could arrange it, yes. But," she added quickly, "I'm sure we haven't got one like that here, Scott, or we'd be knee-deep in casualties by now."

UNDERGRADUATE NOTES: MODULE 4; VIRAL TRICKERY (i). L. HENMAN.
Viruses reinvent themselves all the time. They make tiny changes in their chemistry by mutating. In the case of flu, most humans cope with a new form of the virus because existing antibodies adapt to it. The only penalty is a mild dose of the new form of flu.

But occasionally the virus will mutate in a big way. A drastically new version comes on the scene and existing human antibodies will not know how to deal with it. If the body cannot develop fresh antibodies to tackle the new form, humans are defenceless. That occurred in 1918-19 with the then new swine-flu H1N1 strain that killed tens of millions of people with unprepared immune systems. It was virulent and very fast. If it happened today, someone could get on a train at Milton Keynes feeling vaguely sniffy and he or she could be dead when the train pulls in at Euston, forty-five minutes later. Public health was taken by surprise again in 1957 by Asian flu (H2N2 strain; 1,000,000 deaths) and in 1968 with the arrival of Hong Kong flu (A/H3N2 strain; 700,000 deaths). Another epidemic with a new mutation is long overdue.

Later that day, after she had examined her mice, Laurie reported to Darryl at the hospital. With a victorious grin Laurie declared, "I've done it. I've refined the test. My mice are much more sensitive to the virus than rats. Intravenous injection of a sample that's contaminated with the virus gives the mice nose bleeds in four hours and kills them in five hours flat. Amazing virulence."

Darryl put his hand on her shoulder briefly. "And you're the woman who said she couldn't help because she's not an expert." Then he nodded appreciatively. "That's great. Some good news at last. At least we can speed up the trials now. It's good timing because last night we captured a couple of bats. One male, one female. I want them tested straight away. Come and give the details to the team working here at the hospital." On the way to Microbiology Darryl took a breath and, fearing the worst, asked, "What proportion of the mice die?"

Laurie paused before bringing the bad news.

Her drawn expression and hesitation told him everything. "The lot?"

"Exactly," she answered. "The virus is one hundred per cent fatal."

Megan and Barry Revill strolled peacefully along the bank of the canal on their way to St Mary's Church in Woughton-on-the-Green. They were secure in their belief that the plague would not touch them. In the distance, the monotonous church bells tolled methodically and morbidly.

Four youngsters in scruffy jeans appeared on the opposite towpath, shattering the quiet. They pranced along, paralleling the Revills. The boys traded crude jokes and insults, laughing loudly. Some of the jibes were aimed at Megan and Barry – conveniently close but reassuringly out of reach. Protected from the adults by the ribbon of water, the kids bent down, grabbed stones from the towpath and hurled them towards the couple. They weren't trying to hit the Revills. They were aiming just short so that the stones splashed into the canal, spraying the walkers with water.

"Stop that!" Megan cried.

"Stop that!" the boys echoed with fits of laughter.

"Do something about it, Barry!" Megan insisted.

Ridiculing her, the lads scoffed, "Go on. Do something, Barry."

"There's a bridge coming up," Barry boomed across the water. "I'll be over as soon as we get there," he threatened.

"Oh, we're wetting ourselves," the leading boy jeered. Defiantly, he threw another stone, the largest that he could see. It plunged into the canal just a metre short of the far bank, close to Barry. The dirty water sprinkled over him.

"And we're wetting you," another sniggered.

The sickly child at the back of the pack kept bending down and picking up stones as well. But then he seemed to lose interest. Either he couldn't be bothered to throw them or didn't have the energy to join in. The stones spilled from his floppy fist back to the towpath. Suddenly, he halted, let out an inhuman cry and dropped to the ground. The stones left in his hand rolled pathetically on to the track beside the canal.

On the other side, the Revills sped away, mumbling to each other, "Thank goodness."

Groaning impatiently, the other three boys went back for their fallen friend. A few seconds later, a frightened voice drifted down the waterway. "Mister! Missus! We need help."

Turning her head but not slowing her pace, Mrs Revill shouted, "You should've thought of that before you started throwing stones at us."

*   *   *

The church was nearly full, as if there was to be a wedding or a funeral. But it was the advent of disease that had packed the people in the aisles. In the service, Ross McGavin talked of the need for faith, tolerance, prayer and care in a time of darkness.

"*Though I walk through the valley of the shadow of death, I will fear no evil: for thou art with me; thy rod and thy staff they comfort me*. In our modern hi-tech world, it's tempting to think we can have anything we want. Computers, convenience goods, clever gadgets, children for infertile couples, mobile phones that go off during every sermon, drugs to cure almost all our ills, and weapons with pinpoint accuracy. These days, scientists can even clone life. It's tempting to think we are the masters of the world. But sometimes we're reminded that it's not so. We hear of huge destructive earthquakes, floods, hurricanes and volcanic eruptions. And rampaging disease. These are not the devices of man but of nature. They are visited upon presumptuous people who would think of themselves as masters of God's Earth. Amid our lives of plenty, we also need humility. We *need* a reminder that we cling to life by the thread of God's will. From time to time, we are tested. In such moments we need our faith – our confidence in God – more than anything. *The Lord is my light and my salvation; whom shall I fear? The Lord is the strength of my life; of whom should I be afraid? When the wicked, even my enemies and my foes, came upon me to eat up my flesh, they stumbled and fell.* Let us pray."

Ross McGavin's fears were not for his own safety within the besieged area but for his ability to cope, to explain to good people why they were suffering a cruel punishment, to hide his own incredulity and disillusionment.

After his inadequate sermon, Ross was overwhelmed by a gathering of worried parishioners. They congregated around him like flies swarming to a night light. "Remember, God knows each and every one of us. Our pain is His pain."

When he caught sight of the Revills walking straight past the crowd and heading for the door, Ross called to them, "Megan, Barry? Don't you want to talk to me about the epidemic?"

Megan shook her head. "No, thanks. We

can see you're busy and it's got nothing to do with us."

Ross frowned. He was about to respond but he decided against. First, he had to do his best with the troubled worshippers who were desperate for his help. For the moment, he didn't have the time to take care of the ones who thought that they weren't. He was also concerned about the Hancocks. The most faithful churchgoers in his patch. Surprisingly, Ross hadn't seen them. Why hadn't they come to the service? He prayed that the virus had not touched them.

On the way home, no one bothered Megan and Barry Revill. It was uncannily calm.

Chapter 15

"Negative, negative, negative!" Luckily, there was nothing in striking distance of the frustrated Professor of Biology. Darryl had been told that the cat with the broken leg, the other animals from the veterinary centre, and the bats were blameless. The result from the bats' blood was a particular disappointment to him. The blood hadn't infected experimental mice. Not even after eight hours. Undoubtedly negative.

"Do you know how many people we've got in Isolation?" he exclaimed.

The two technicians in Microbiology shrugged helplessly. They'd worked non-stop. They hadn't had time to keep up with the casualty figures and they couldn't be blamed for the viral source being so elusive.

"Three dead and eleven dying. A lot of them happen to be kids. The youngest so far is a boy of four. The latest, a boy of ten, collapsed by the canal. He could have fallen in and drowned. If you saw him now, drowning internally in blood, you'd wish he had. And that's not the end of it. I bet there are people living on their own – or scared families who keep to themselves – who are dying on their own, unknown to us. On top of that, I've just been told there's still no link between the first two victims, Oliver Church and Tammy Smith, never mind the rest." Darryl exhaled loudly. "Sorry," he said. "It's not your fault." He shook his head sadly. Deprived of sleep and positive results, he looked haggard. His tiredness was not improving his temper. "I got a verdict from the CDC in America as well." He slapped a brief fax message and read, "Most closely related to Machupo haemorrhagic fever but not the same. More than two hundred viral antibody types screened. Your strain not in our register. Suggest you have a mutated one. Therefore, no cures or vaccines available." He sighed and said, "The message ends with 'Good luck'. We'll need it."

More negatives.

The phone in his pocket trilled. It was the Head of Security calling. "No," Darryl said after listening for a couple of minutes. "If it's up to me to decide, we don't confirm or deny the rumour. If we confirm someone was shot trying to escape, people might panic. If we deny it, someone'll think the soldiers won't shoot and then try to get out themselves. Just let the rumour fester. If they think someone's been shot, they'll be worried. It'll keep them in their place." He went quiet for a while and then finished by saying, "I don't honestly care a great deal about the press. Tell them you can't deny it or confirm it. They'll make up their own story anyway."

Darryl turned to his technicians and said, "Good work. Keep on looking. We've got to identify the source before the hospital turns into a death camp." He hurried away.

Scott found his mother asleep on the sofa at home. She looked exhausted but she stirred when he went up to her. He bent down and shook her gently, whispering, "Mum? Are you all right?" When he straightened up, there was a dreadful ache in his back and the top of his legs. The aspirin had helped his headache but his other aches and pains refused to budge.

Laurie jumped, sat up and for a second seemed confused about where she was.

"It's OK," Scott said. "Just me. You're home."

His mother relaxed and wiped her eyes. She let out a long breath and muttered, "Asleep, I get terrible dreams about . . . people getting infected. Awake, it's a *real* nightmare. There's no getting away from it."

Immediately, Scott realized who had featured in her dream. It was her hesitation that told him. "You mean you dreamed about me getting the virus?"

"I need a nice, normal shower. One that doesn't demolish the top layer of skin." Looking up at her son, she said, "As long as it stays just a dream."

"I'm more interested in the real nightmare," Scott responded. "Any news?"

"I've confirmed it's a hot virus."

Scott queried, "A hot virus? What does that mean?"

"It kills quickly and its strike rate in mice is one hundred per cent. Our best hope is that it's not a hundred per cent lethal in people. We need it to pick on one hardy individual who'll survive. Then we'll have some blood to work with. We'll have antibodies. That one person will save himself or herself and then the rest of us by giving us serum to work with. Until then. . ." She stood up, stretched and put out her arms. "I've got a hundred and one insects to test." With sarcasm she said, "It's great fun, mashing up flies and injecting the goo into mice to see if they get sick. And I'm trying to isolate the virus. That's vital. Then we can test out treatments on it, but . . . I need to get a pure sample first."

"First," Scott said, "you need that shower. You smell of Dettol. Do you want me to get a meal on?"

"That would be wonderful. What's on the menu?"

"Tinned stuff or other tinned stuff."

"Mmm. Sounds delicious. See you soon."

At Heather's place, Darryl relaxed for a few short hours. "You deserve a break," Heather claimed. "You can't expect to keep up the frantic pace *and* be effective."

Lounging in a comfortable armchair, Darryl grinned. "You sound like a mother-hen. Or a midwife talking to a new mother." When

Heather handed him a mug of strong black coffee, he said, "You haven't exactly been dawdling yourself."

Cheekily, she replied, "Oh, you noticed, then."

"I notice, yes. But sometimes I don't get the chance to comment on it or to thank you. You and the rest of the team. I only have time to blow up at the frustrations." Looking round the modest living room and changing the subject, he said, "It was good of you to let me share your place. Good company."

Heather smiled. "Thanks. But anything would seem like luxury compared to working at the hospital right now."

Sombre, Darryl asked her, "Who've you got on the other side of the fence, Heather? Who are you cut off from?"

"No one, really. Not much of a close family."

"Not a boyfriend?"

She shook her head. "How about you?"

Darryl didn't respond immediately. He stared into his mug for a few seconds, put it down on a table mat, reached into his shirt pocket and pulled out a small photograph. He held it out to Heather.

She examined the photo and then Darryl's face. "A boy? Your son?"

He nodded. "Same age as our youngest victim. Four."

"Sorry, Darryl. It must be hard. . ." Realizing that her sympathy wasn't going to help, she said instead, "He's a good-looking lad. He must be missing you. What's his name?"

"Mark." Darryl pocketed the prized photograph.

"I guess that means his mum's out there as well," Heather said.

"Sort of," Darryl answered. "I don't know where she is. She . . . er . . . thought that motherhood didn't suit her. It interfered with her lifestyle."

"Who's looking after Mark?"

"My mother and father."

"You'd better take good care of yourself, Darryl. Mark'll need you."

"Yeah, I know." He took a swig of coffee and added, "A lot of kids need me right now." At once, he sat up straight in the chair, startled. "I reckon it's an arbovirus," he uttered.

"A what?"

"Arbovirus. It comes from arthropod-borne. Take the first two letters of each word. It means an insect-borne virus."

"Why say that? You haven't got any evidence, have you?"

"No," he answered. "But I should've seen it before. We've got lots of kids with the virus. They tend to play outside more – in grassy or watery places where they come into contact with plenty of insects. Kids get bitten more." He stopped talking, his brain clearly in overdrive.

"What's up?"

"I haven't been thinking straight," he proclaimed, grabbing his phone and dialling Microbiology. "Darryl," he announced curtly once he got through. "Those bats we caught. You tested their blood. What about their droppings?" He listened for a few seconds. "Well, get the team out for fresh bats or fresh droppings and then test it pronto."

"What's on your mind?" Heather asked when he put the phone away.

"Bats are great guzzlers of insects. If we *have* got an arbovirus, the bats will surely have eaten some carrier insects. But their blood's clean. So where's the virus gone to? If they swallow it but don't take it into their bloodstream, it must pass straight through them. See what I mean? They must excrete it.

It's one way to check if we've got an insect-borne virus. If I'm right, bat droppings should be contaminated."

Amy Hancock didn't kill her mother but she did suffocate her little brother. With tears in her eyes and anguish on her face, she pressed the pillow on to his poor bloodshot face. "Bless him, Lord Jesus," she murmured. "Have mercy on him. And me." She couldn't allow him to go through the same agony as her mum and dad. He was only tiny. He didn't understand pain and he didn't deserve such a death. While she held the pillow, she thought of her mum's last words. "Don't let him suffer, Amy. Please don't let him suffer." Her mother had fought the disease, the pain and exhaustion to stammer those few crucial words.

Amy could not let her mother down. She had promised. She kept her hands on the white pillow while her tears spattered it.

Her mum and dad had both fallen ill at the same time. They hadn't been able to help each other. Amy hadn't known what to do. Whenever her parents managed to talk through their suffering, they told her, "Just pray, Amy. We'll be fine. We're in God's hands." They had never trusted doctors. They placed all their trust in God.

If Amy could have her time again and if she'd been brave enough, she would've smothered her parents as well. Anything but that bloody sickness. But Amy didn't think of herself as brave and she didn't want her time again. Not this particular time, anyway. It was the worst time of her short life.

She put the pillow aside. Her brother was at peace. She had denied the heartless virus. It would not possess his ailing body. She looked down at her murderous hands and noticed some of his blood on them. She washed it off carefully into a bowl, then took the water outside and poured it lovingly on a rose bush in their back garden. In a way, her brother would live on in the flower.

Spent, Amy sat on the lawn and cuddled her pet rabbit. Now, they were the only ones left in the family.

It was in the garden that Ross McGavin found Amy and her pet rabbit when he burst into their Passmore home. He was too late to do anything for Mr and Mrs Hancock and their baby. He could only sit with Amy, hug her, cry with her.

And, in his head, Ross heard some unwelcome and uninvited words. *My God, my God, why hast thou forsaken me? Why art thou so far from helping me, and from the words of my roaring?* Where was his confidence now?

As far as Syreeta knew, she was the only journalist trapped inside the cordon. In her mind, a golden opportunity swamped all other images. Danger, her own health, other people's grief and sensitivity. All of these took second place behind her good fortune. While her competitors filed their reports from the outside and pictured the scene from behind razor wire, she had the inside story and the close-ups. She could get to the heart of the tragedy. She could scoop the big prizes.

Syreeta got as close as possible to the hospital entrance. A long-range lens took care of the rest. And there was another advantage of hanging around the stricken hospital. When an ambulance roared away from the site, she followed. The area that it served was so restricted that she could usually discover where it had gone in time to get the pictures that mattered. She could usually talk to neighbours, relatives and bystanders to get the stories that mattered. Armed with camera and notebook, she trampled all over people's anguish in the name of public interest.

Darryl looked more upbeat. He'd spotted a pinprick of light at the end of his long, dark tunnel. He'd got his arbovirus theory and he had a tantalizing new patient. A little girl called Amy Hancock had come in from Passmore, along with her pet rabbit. A vicar had found them and alerted the authorities. Considering that the whole of the rest of her family had succumbed to the virus and that she'd been cooped up with them, tending to them, it struck Darryl as remarkable that Amy and her rabbit seem physically well. She must have touched their blood or fluids. "I want her under twenty-four-hour-a-day observation," he told the ward sister. "And the rabbit. Can you call Dr Henman at the university? She'll take on the rabbit."

"Amy won't be parted from her pet," the sister said. "She's still in shock."

"No problem," Darryl replied. "After what she's been through, I wouldn't dream of separating them if Amy doesn't want to. Get someone to fetch the rabbit's hutch from her house and let her keep it in the ward."

The nurse looked doubtful. "We're not exactly set up for rabbits," she pointed out. "What about food, for example?"

"Catering will have to be creative. Besides, a lot of food they dish up to the human patients is rabbit food." Seriously, he continued, "Right now, Amy and the rabbit get star treatment. OK? Either of them might have precisely what we need: immunity to the virus. Resistant individuals come in all shapes and sizes. Even a small vulnerable girl could be our saviour. Take a blood sample as soon as you think she's up to it."

The sister lowered her voice and said, "You know the baby who died – Amy's brother – the disease hadn't gone far enough to kill him. An autopsy will. . ."

Darryl held up his hand to stop her. "I heard. I want the autopsy cancelled. We don't have the time and resource. No one wants to know the results. Do you understand what I mean?" In a whisper, he said, "What's the point of providing the police with evidence to bring a murder charge? If Amy's done what you and I think she's done, she deserves a medal for bravery, not blame. If it came to it, I'm not sure I'd have the guts to put a loved one out of his misery. No, there's only one murderer here: the virus. The baby had the disease and the disease kills. End of story. He's infected so I want him cremated immediately. Agreed?"

The sister nodded. "It's not the proper procedure but I'll get on to it — using your authority."

"Just do it. There's a time and a place for proper procedure and this isn't it. I'll sign the death certificate giving the cause as haemorrhagic fever."

Chapter 16

No way to Boots, no way to school. Lucy and Rev were hanging out by the twenty-four-hour shop in Tinkers Bridge. They were watching the commotion at the end of the street where it met Groveway and the wire barricade. There was a delivery of goods and newspapers. Soldiers were hurling sacks, boxes and bundles over the barrier as if they were throwing pieces of meat into a lions' den. A couple of helpers from the store were picking them up on this side of the boundary and ferrying them into the back of the shop.

On the rough ground to the side of the store, the dirt was really flying. A gang of boys rushed up and down on the dry earth, chasing a football. The cloud wasn't just dust. The lads also kicked up and scattered insects that nipped their bare legs.

Rev's eyes lit up when he saw the lead story in the new edition of the local paper. He murmured to himself, "That's something for Mum."

"What are you mumbling about?" asked Lucy.

He took her arm and said, "I've got an idea. Why don't you come back to my place. We could. . ."

Lucy's expression stopped him in his tracks. "From what I've heard of your parents, that'd be asking for trouble."

"A little bit more trouble won't be noticeable in a crisis. Besides," he added, "why *should* I have to keep you secret?"

"I'm not going to put you up if she chucks you out," Lucy warned him with a grin.

"Come on, Darwin," Rev said to the beagle.

On their way through Passmore, they came to a stop outside one particular house. Lucy spotted a couple of boys secreted in the side alley, just about to climb over the tall gate into the private back garden. "What are *they* doing here?" she said to herself. "Up to no good."

Rev frowned. "I think that's. . ." He glanced

at the newspaper. The front page carried a photograph of a bewildered girl, clutching a rabbit, being led out of the Hancocks' house. "Yes, it's where the new victims live. Or did live. They won't be in. Most of them are dead."

"Typical!" Lucy hissed. "They're doing a bit of looting." With her hands on her hips, she shouted at the top of her voice, "Gary Davenport! Come out of there!"

"Shush," one of the boys called back.

"Don't you shush me, Tony!" Lucy replied. "Do you want me to call the police?"

Sheepishly, the two lads filed out of the alley.

"You should be ashamed," she began her lecture. She was at least ten centimetres shorter than the boys but, totally fearless, she weighed straight in to them. "You saw the picture in the paper and didn't waste any time, I mean, coming round to break in."

Tony tried to defend himself. "Steamin' idea. They don't need stuff no more."

"It don't belong to you," Lucy stated.

"It belongs to a little girl called Amy, according to this," Rev put in, pointing to the pathetic picture in the newspaper. "The only one alive."

"You keep out of this!" Tony said angrily. "Just watch yourself." He walked up to Rev as if to land a head-butt on him.

Darwin didn't help. The nervous dog didn't bark ferociously but backed away.

Lucy administered a heavy kick to the boy's backside and said, "Forget it, Tony. Go home or I'll tell your mum what you're up to. Then you'll get more than a boot on the bum."

Tony tore himself away from Rev's face and looked down severely at Lucy. He could see that she meant it. He considered retaliation only for a split-second then he caved in. "All right," he muttered.

"Anyway," Gary said, "the whole street's seen us now. Look at the posh curtains twitching, thanks to you," he snarled at Lucy. "We won't forget this."

"Neither will I," Lucy said to the retreating boys.

As soon as he walked into his own lounge, Rev blurted out the news and held up the headline: PASSMORE IS NEXT TO SUFFER. Under-neath there was a fictitious quotation. *"Now I'm all alone," says Amy.*

Megan screeched, "A Passmore family!"

"A good, clean-living, God-fearing, vandal-free Passmore family," Rev replied with a certain amount of glee. "The Hancocks." He tossed the newspaper on to the seat beside her. He wasn't rejoicing in the Hancocks' fate but in the blow to his mother's pomposity.

Megan ignored the report. Instead, she looked up at Lucy with disdain. "Who's this?" she said. The girl didn't look right at all. Her clothes were shabby, her hair uncultured, her glasses cheap, and her figure. . . She hadn't been eating the right foods at all. The girl must have a diet of crisps and chocolate.

For a moment, Rev could imagine his mother holding out a crucifix to keep the Tinkers Bridge demon at bay. "This is Lucy," he announced. "A friend of mine."

"Friend? What does that mean?"

"A friend?" he replied. "It's someone you go around with because you like their company, because you get on well. It's someone you bring home sometimes."

Turning her stare on her son, she said, "If I need a definition, I'll use a dictionary."

"We're going upstairs to listen to a few CDs."

His mum was so shocked that she hadn't

managed a reply before they disappeared from the room.

But a minute later, Lucy was yelling at Rev, "If I'm just a tool, I'm not staying."

"A tool?" Rev queried.

"I mean, a hammer for you to batter your mother with. I'm not playing that sort of game." Deep down, Lucy knew that she loved Rev. But he could be a bit of an oaf. And she had quite a temper. She stormed downstairs and out of the house.

When Rev followed, his mum's words brought him to a halt. "I'm not sure a girl like *that*'s welcome in this house."

"No?" Rev shouted angrily. "Pity. She's just been a great friend to the Hancocks."

MICROBIOLOGY LAB NOTES: SUMMARY.
A batch of fifteen mice was infected using blood from virus patient, F6. To five of the mice, Amy Hancock's serum – possibly containing antibodies – was also administered. If Hancock is immune, her antibodies would slow the disease in those mice. Another five of the mice were injected with the serum from Hancock's rabbit. Again, any antibodies would inhibit progress of the disease. Result: all

fifteen mice died from haemorrhagic fever in four to six hours. Statistically, there was no significant difference between the rates of disease progression. Conclusion: Hancock and the rabbit do not have antibodies. Either they are in the incubation stage of the disease themselves, prior to symptoms, or neither Hancock nor the rabbit caught the virus in the first place.

Additional information. Blood from Amy Hancock does not cause haemorrhagic fever in mice after six hours. Conclusion: she is not infected with the virus but she cannot supply antibodies.

The crimson tide began to turn in Darryl's favour a day after the good news that Amy Hancock was not going to become ill and the bad news that she wasn't capable of curing anyone.

First, some of the bat droppings gave a positive result. Helping the technicians in the microbiology lab at the hospital, Darryl showed that the virus was lurking in one out of five samples. A few bats must have eaten something that carried the microbes. Darryl reasoned that it had to be an insect but not one of their main prey, otherwise more samples would have been positive. Then came the telephone call from Laurie. She sounded triumphant but weary. "Gnats," she pronounced. "It's carried by gnats."

"Are you absolutely sure?"

"Crush ten gnats, inject into mice and they die from haemorrhagic fever in five hours. We've cracked it, Darryl!"

"Great stuff," he responded. "Well done. And it fits some results I've just got on bat droppings. We're on our way at last. I can't linger now, Laurie. I must make some urgent calls. Thanks again." He rang off and immediately dialled another number. "Right. We're in business. Get me a light aircraft upstairs spraying insecticide over the quarantine area. Preferably use a chemical that's safe for human exposure, but killing gnats is the first priority. I'd rather treat people with pesticide overdoses than haemorrhagic fever."

Straight away, he organized for a driver to go out and announce with a megaphone what would soon happen. He rushed to write a notice to go out to all households, telling them that they were about to be sprayed with insecticide, at least twice. Darryl had to wait for the hazard assessment on the chosen chemical before he could add precise precautions to the information but he guessed that everyone would have to make sure they were inside with the windows shut when the cloud of pesticide descended on them. Suddenly hyperactive, Darryl called the woman who was in charge of delivering supplies. "I need as many domestic fly sprays as you've got. Yes. A few thousand aerosols – as long as they work on gnats. Don't spare the ozone hole. Put in insect repellent creams as well. Anything you can get hold of. Every house should get something. And contact an animal centre. I want to import every known animal, bird or insect that feeds on gnats. I want herds of them delivered straight after I give the gnats a dose of chemical warfare. The predators can mop up any survivors, wiping out every gnat in the area." He also called the hospital manager. After he'd explained what he was going to do, he said, "There's bound to be some allergic reactions. In a few thousand people, they'll be a small percentage who are sensitive to the pesticide. Get the hospital and health centre on standby to handle it, will you? You must have allergy and anaphylactic shock specialists. Make sure they're ready for action. They might have quite a bit of work soon."

"Gnats? That's brilliant," Scott said enthusiastically to his mum on a rare visit home. "You're a genius, Dr Henman. We kill the gnats off and that's the end of that."

Laurie did not want to bring him down but she had to shake her head. "Two things," she said. "It's not easy to destroy all the midges and it might be impossible. I'm sure Darryl's running round right now with a fly swat, doing what he can. But, it's only one piece of the jigsaw, I'm afraid. They can't be the original source. Gnats can't suddenly become carriers without something giving them the virus. Where did they get it from?"

Scott shuffled uncomfortably in his chair. "Spoil-sport," he muttered. He felt very tired and he put it down to not sleeping well because of his mum's erratic schedule and his worries about her safety.

"If we exterminate all the gnats but don't locate the original source," she explained, "it'll break out again with a different carrier or with a new generation of gnats that eventually fly into the area. No, we still need to find and eliminate the cause."

UNDERGRADUATE NOTES: MODULE 4; VIRAL TRICKERY (ii). L. HENMAN.
The smallpox virus killed forty per cent of those who succumbed to it. The disease devastated the heart, kidneys and brain. Survivors had kidney damage, horribly disfigured faces, and were frequently blind. The last reported case of smallpox was in 1978. It has been eradicated by vaccination – the first disease to have been wiped out by humans. [Archaeologists should still be immunized against smallpox because they might encounter ancient mummies that still harbour a viable smallpox virus.] Why are we so poor at eradicating other viral diseases? Smallpox was unique. It could be tackled successfully because it had only one natural reservoir: human beings. It could not hide in other species like mice, mosquitoes and monkeys. Remove it from the human population and it was removed completely. Most viruses hide in a carrier, called a vector, in which they cause no harm. These vectors

are hard to find and even harder to eliminate. Somewhere, a virus will lurk even if humans are freed from the disease. Sooner or later, it will re-emerge and attack humans once again.

Biting insects are a particularly convenient carrier for viruses because their behaviour ideally suits the spreading of microbes. Blood-feeding insects bite into human flesh and spit into the wound a chemical cocktail that (a) prevents the blood from clotting, (b) opens up (dilates) the capillaries, and (c) fends off human antibodies while they feast on an unobstructed stream of blood. This is a perfect medium also for bacteria and viruses. They multiply in the insect, get into its salivary gland and are then injected directly into human blood while the insect is taking its meal. They too appreciate a steady flow of blood.

Chapter 17

High noon. It was hot and sultry. The prison camp appeared to be deserted. The streets were empty as if the people were expecting a gunfight or an attack. At midday exactly, a siren sounded, making it seem even more like imminent war. In this battle, though, buzzing insects were the enemy, the bomb would be a chemical weapon, and people used their own homes as air-raid shelters. Soon an organo-phosphate chemical would descend from the sky. It was deadly to insects, harmful to some humans. The ring of soldiers had retreated temporarily to safe positions.

First there was the distant drone of the aircraft. Instead of sheltering under tables, residents gathered at their windows and watched with fingers crossed. Then, suddenly the aeroplane swooped out of the eastern sky like a giant mechanical bat seeking its insect prey. Starting at the university, just metres above the rooftops, it opened its tanks and a fine white spray emerged from the length of both wings. Slowly, the white cloud drifted down and blanketed a strip of the restricted area. At the western edge of quarantine zone, the aeroplane stopped spraying, lurched upwards and turned 180 degrees. It came down on its second run and saturated another belt of land with choking insecticide.

In his house, Aaron Wishart looked out and smiled. It was about time that the Government did something about all the flies. Horrible, un-hygienic things. Hatched on moist manure and rubbish and rotting corpses, scavenging on sewage and garbage and putrid flesh, carrying the dirt on their bristling body hair and padded feet and sticky tongues, landing on clean food and polluting it with their filth, passing on germs and disease. Extermination was the only answer. Good riddance to the lot of them. The mere thought of the utterly unspeakable be-haviour of flies made Aaron feel dirty. He went upstairs to take a vigorous scalding shower.

For a minute, Syreeta opened the window of her front room. Holding her breath, she poked her camera outside and aimed it upwards as if she were shooting down the aeroplane. But she was only shooting a photograph: another scoop, another award winner. It would look great on the front page of the local paper. She ran out of air, closed the window and coughed twice. Then she smiled. The picture would be worth the risk.

The bombing raids continued to release insecticide in bands running parallel to H7 and H9. The aeroplane came from the east and the west alternately, like a lawnmower creating precise stripes of light and dark on a football pitch. Once it had completed the last run beside H7 Chaffron Way, just beyond the hospital, the aircraft made two extra runs, perpendicular to the others. It followed the course of the canal and then the river, scattering an extra dose on the waterways and the wet grasslands that harboured millions of insects. Then the aircraft retreated to restock its tanks. In its wake, fine white particles hung in the air like a fog for a while before settling on every surface in the dormant diseased sector. Any flying insect landing on it would absorb the poison through its feet and die. The plane would return later in the day to pursue its relentless war on insects with a second treatment. At dusk – that time when midges saturated the air in a hunt for human blood – the whole process would be repeated.

The fight back had begun.

While pesticide engulfed the place, the agonizing and gory blood-bath continued in Isolation. Luckily, death came quickly in the guise of heart failure, shock due to blood loss, or drowning through lung congestion. The staff did everything they could to make sure that infected mucus and blood did not land on another person because, if it did, the cycle of disease would almost certainly begin again.

Two porters wearing protective suits and masks were loading the latest victim, her bed-linen, her belongings and her clothes into a casket. They would seal the wooden box, go through decontamination, and then wheel it on a trolley to the incinerator. In the hospital they were used to handling death but this was in a league of its own. Even after trauma counselling, the porters would be scarred for the rest of their lives by their experience.

By the next bed, a young nurse called Daljit reached up with her double latex surgical gloves and changed the drip for the ten-year-old. The nutrients gave his vital organs a chance of functioning just a bit longer in the face of the viral onslaught. If they did, maybe his exhausted immune system would buy that bit of time to adjust to the infection and make an effective antibody. It would need only one successful response to the invader and, within hours, his blood serum would be saving other patients and inoculating the unaffected. The nurse looked down at the sick boy. She tried to persuade herself that he would be the one. That way, her time and energy would not be wasted. She would be helping this fallen angel to live again and she would be helping to cure everyone else. But she had to struggle to conjure up such optimism. In the face of haemorrhagic fever, everything was a struggle. As yet, the boy showed no sign of recovery. He showed every sign of following the others. The tear in the corner of Daljit's eye was perfectly formed from clear salty water. The boy's was altogether different.

Outside, the organophosphate got to work.

Once absorbed into an insect, it played havoc with the creature's nervous system. The cruel chemical made nerve impulses fire all the time. Constantly switched on, every muscle went into spasm. The heart, legs, wings, everything went berserk, until the insect died from nervous overload.

The organophosphate did much the same to people but it was less toxic to human beings. Even so, there were some casualties. There were cases of trembling hands and feet, flickering eyelids and twitching faces, breathing difficulties, stomach cramps, violent rages and one heart attack. Two people – a young asthmatic and an old man with a weak heart – did not respond to treatment. They became the terrible price that had to be paid to eliminate the gnats.

MICROBIOLOGY LAB NOTES: ISOLATION OF VIRUS; SUMMARY.
CAUTION: ALL OF THE FOLLOWING STEPS ARE EXTREMELY HAZARDOUS. BIOSAFETY LEVEL 4 IS REQUIRED THROUGHOUT THE PROCEDURE. Grow infected human red blood cells in petri dishes. Mix cells with ammonium sulphate solution.

Decant water layer from the solids that settle. Warning: the solid contains the virus. Mix the solid with ethanol and spin at low speed in a centrifuge to collect waste cell fragments. Pour off liquid and spin at very high speed to collect a pellet of virus. Warning: this is a highly concentrated and nearly pure sample. Finally, separate the virus from extraneous matter by size exclusion chromatography. ALL WASTE AND IMPURITIES TO BE COLLECTED AND INCINERATED. Detailed procedure follows.

Laurie's spine was still tingling when she finally cleared decontamination and Darryl arrived at the university. "I've isolated the virus, got a snap of it!" she announced triumphantly.

Darryl said, "Really? Let me see."

Laurie sat at a computer and said, "This is on-line to the electron microscope which is behind enemy lines." She nodded towards the high-containment facility. "I'll show you what you'd be seeing if you were in there." She tapped a few keys.

The screen came alive with a black and white image of evil, made visible by the hi-tech microscope. Magnified more than 100,000 times, the virus revealed itself as a long, thin and fuzzy shape, like a short piece of thread. The viruses in view writhed in front of Laurie and Darryl, sometimes coiling up into spirals. They swam around randomly, tumbling and slithering chaotically like an endless rush-hour of frantic pushing and shoving. A cell that had been overrun with the virus looked like a ghastly bowl of wriggling worms.

"Ugly little buggers, aren't they?" Darryl hissed. He wagged his finger at the screen. "Now I know what you look like, I'm on your tail." He looked at Laurie and said, "Terrific work. If I could get you promoted to Professor, I would. Anyway, hit it with interferon, AZT, protease inhibitors, ribovirin and anything else you can lay your hands on. Let's see how it reacts to antivirals."

It was late. The time when things really began to happen. A party perhaps, or a night club. But no one was in the mood to party and there were no night clubs within this prison. Besides, Scott just wanted to go home. He'd had enough. His limbs and head felt heavy, his muscles ached. His worries about his mother and the virus, his lack of sleep, were getting him down. He longed for normal life again.

Even after the chemical assault on its carrier, the diminutive virus still loomed large in Milton Keynes. It dominated everything. It hijacked every conversation. Scott said to Rev, "You know, it's the closest thing I can think of to pure evil. You name something else that's really grim and nasty and deadly and I bet I'll find something nice to say about it. I'll find its good side. But I can't think of anything nice to say about a virus."

"How about nuclear weapons?"

"Pretty nasty, yeah, but some people say they're so nasty, we're too scared to use them. So, they've kept the peace."

Rev thought about it for a moment. "How about the great white shark? That's what I call a nasty piece of work. Did you see *Jaws*?"

Scott nodded. "The one in the film was evil, that's for sure. But really, sharks only attack to eat or to defend their territory. They don't do it to excess. They're sleek and I imagine they're nice to their kids. A virus isn't even alive. It only gets a life by taking over another creature and producing billions and billions of clones of itself, not caring about its host. Where's its saving grace? I'll tell you. It hasn't got one. Pure evil."

Rev took a gulp from his can of drink. "You're in a right old mood tonight."

"Have you made it up to Lucy?" Scott asked.

"Haven't seen her since she walked out on me this morning. But . . . I don't know. I'll go and see her tomorrow. See how things stand." He paused and then added, "Girls. They're a different species, aren't they? Totally alien." Suddenly, he put down his drink. "That's it!" he exclaimed.

"What is?"

"The alien in *Alien*. The one that dripped gore and grew inside humans, then burst out through the stomach. That's a bit like our virus, only bigger. Evil or what?"

"Evil – and fictional," Scott replied. "That stuff in films isn't real, Rev. Our virus, it's staring us in the face. And we don't know who's already infected. We can only wait to find out."

Chapter 18

Laurie worked through the night. Her battle against the virus put the rest of her life in perspective. The invisible invasion sifted the trivial from the important. Her next promotion and increase in salary, her academic reputation, the maintenance of a big house – all became inconsequential. The well-being of her son, herself and her neighbours, and her ability to fight the disease – suddenly these took precedence. Caring was what really mattered.

But by dawn she was frustrated. "I've blasted it with every antiviral in the book," she reported to Darryl by phone. Her free hand ran through her hair, tugging compulsively at the roots. "Interferon, AZT, DDI, protease inhibitors, gangcyclovir, acyclovir, ribovirin. That's the lot. Nothing. I can almost hear this virus laughing at me."

Darryl did not reply immediately but he murmured, "Damn." There was a noise like a sigh and then he said, "And we haven't cracked the original source yet. We don't know where the gnats got it from." He was not just baffled but tired and impatient.

"Everything looked good. I thought we had it on the run." Laurie shook her head.

"The thing's devious to say the least – or I'm plain stupid, not seeing what's under our noses." He hesitated before saying, "You gave it your best shot, Laurie. Go home and get a bit of sleep. You deserve it. I'll get back to you when you can help some more."

"What about you?"

With humour, he answered, "I don't deserve a rest – not till I've got it beat. The nurses here'll pump me with stimulants to keep me going."

Laurie cleared up, finished making her written notes on the futile overnight experiments, and trudged home along the path by the river. The air was eerily and pleasantly free of insects.

* * *

Laurie sat on the edge of her son's bed and tilted her head. "Are you sure you're feeling OK?" she said anxiously.

Still groggy, Scott mumbled. "I'm fine. Just . . . I don't know . . . unsettled with all this going on. And it's only seven-thirty, Mum. Us young folk don't come alive till eleven, you know."

Laurie smiled. "I know. Eleven at night."

Before she went to lie down, Laurie had some breakfast. Scott took some paracetamol and then joined her, still in his night clothes.

She looked at her watch and commented, "Not eleven yet."

"Yeah, well, once you woke me up, I might as well get on with it. Any news on the virus? Have you kicked its ass some more?"

Plainly, his tired mother wanted to be upbeat but she was very disappointed. "I can see it now. I got an electron micrograph of it. It's like tiny worms. But that's all I've done, provided a portrait we can all hang in a prominent position in our homes. I've tried every antiviral drug we've got and it ignores them all. So, my only achievement is the picture. Now, I can see the virus wriggling away even when I close my eyes. I can see them in the lab, in my dreams, anywhere. Great."

"Can't you identify the wee beastie now you've got its mug shot?"

Laurie shook her head. She sipped some tea and said, "It's a totally new one, never been seen before. Our American contacts say it's a cousin of Bolivian haemorrhagic fever, otherwise known as Machupo, but it's not the same."

Scott nearly knocked his bowl off the table. "Did you say Bolivian?"

Suddenly alert again despite her fatigue, Laurie stared at her son. "What? Do you know something, Scott?"

His mouth was open and he struggled to swallow. Eventually the shocked words came out. "I think you'd better talk to the Revills about their dog."

Laurie flew back to work and gathered all of the equipment she needed. Gloves, syringe, sealed vials. It was mid-morning before she rang the Revills' bell and whispered to Scott, "Remember, whatever you do, don't touch the dog."

The atmosphere inside the house resembled a fridge. There was Barry and Megan, grumpy, barely saying a word to Rev who had brought Lucy home again. Lucy had insisted. She was not there to create the atmosphere but to try and do something about it, to show Rev's mum and dad that she was a life form higher than the virus. Darwin was lying between them all, stretched out in oblivious luxury.

Looking nervously at the beagle, Laurie began, "I'm here because of Darwin. He came from Bolivia, didn't he?"

Megan seemed reluctant to admit to anything as if she knew that their neighbour was about to denounce Darwin when it was obvious that the horrible disease came from somewhere else. "Yes," she said, more like a question than an answer.

Laurie didn't have the time or patience to approach the subject delicately and diplomatically. "There's a real chance that the virus comes from Bolivia," she announced.

"What are you saying?" Megan cried, knowing perfectly well. She called Darwin over to sit beside her and put both arms round his neck protectively. The dog licked her.

"That's very unwise, Megan. In fact, as we sit here, we might all be in considerable danger."

"No, we're not! We're a good clean family, including Darwin. We took him to the vet – just in case he had fleas. They'd have noticed any problems. And he's been well and truly checked in quarantine."

"They look out for the obvious: rabies and that sort of thing, not rare viruses. Besides, if he's the carrier, it won't have any effect on him. He's perfectly healthy. It doesn't mean we won't cop it by coming into contact with his urine or faeces."

"I told you, we're clean, not like. . ."

Lucy dared to interrupt before she heard something that would make her very angry. "Which vet did you take him to, Mrs Revill?"

Megan could not force herself to respond to this tramp from Tinkers Bridge so Barry answered, "The animal centre in Woughton."

Lucy nodded and looked directly at Laurie when she said, "The one where Tammy Smith worked."

Laurie looked puzzled. She'd heard that Darryl's researchers had followed up every animal that had been to the centre. "Was there a record of his visit?"

"I don't know," Barry replied. "It didn't bother us. But we didn't even get to see the vet. A helper took a quick look and suggested a powder for fleas. That was it. Perhaps that didn't warrant an entry in the log book, register or whatever it is."

"This is very important," Laurie said, leaning forward. "Did he do anything on the floor? I think you know what I mean."

Barry glanced at his wife before answering. "He got nervous while he was being examined, I'm afraid."

"Urine?"

Barry nodded as if he couldn't let the word pass his lips.

"Who cleared it up?"

"An assistant – a young girl."

"Tammy," Laurie murmured. "When was this?"

Barry thought about it. "Two to three weeks ago."

To Laurie, it made sense. Tammy died exactly a week ago. So, if she'd been exposed to the virus when she contacted Darwin's urine, she would have incubated the virus for a week, then succumbed to flu-like symptoms for a couple of days and followed that with two days of bleeding before yielding to the disease. From beginning to end: ten or eleven days. The abruptness of it all chilled her.

Urgently, Laurie asked, "Do you know Oliver Church?"

"No."

"There's *got* to be a connection," Laurie muttered to herself. "Have you had any odd jobs done on the house?"

"No."

"Hang on," Rev put in. "Didn't you call in a carpet cleaner to clear up after Darwin?"

Laurie leapt in. "Who was it? What company?"

"No one from Tinkers Bridge, that's for sure," Megan stated.

"It was someone called Carpet Care, out in Milton Keynes Village. They said they were busy but they could sort it out."

"What was the name of the person who came?"

"I've no idea," Barry replied.

Laurie recalled the timing of those first two deaths. She was sure that Oliver Church died three days before Tammy. "Did the carpet cleaner come here three days before you took Darwin to the animal centre?" she asked.

"Er . . . something like that," Barry said. "A couple of days, I think."

Laurie muttered to herself, "Close enough." Aloud she asked, "Can I use your phone?"

Barry shrugged.

The receptionist at Carpet Care made a clicking noise with her tongue while she checked the company's records. "Yes," she said, putting an end to the quiet tutting. "Nearly three weeks ago. Mr Revill in Passmore."

"Who did the job?" asked Laurie.

"Ah. That was a bit awkward. You see, we'd got a rush on. We used a sub-contractor."

"Who?"

"Someone in the locality. We've used him before. His name's Phil Trafford, Tinkers Bridge."

"Not Oliver Church?"

"I can't say I've heard of anyone with that name."

"Oh, well. Thanks for your help." Laurie rang off, sighed and commented, "Sounds like you got someone called Phil Trafford, not Oliver."

"I wouldn't bank on it," Lucy put in. When they all turned to look at her, Lucy declared, "I mean, Oliver Church worked with Phil."

"Are you sure?"

"Yes. I'll phone and see if he did the job if you like," Lucy answered.

Laurie handed the phone to Lucy without asking Rev's parents for permission. The occasion no longer warranted niceties.

Three minutes later, they had the answer. On the day that Darwin soiled the Revills' carpet, Phil was busy. He sent his partner, Oliver, to do the steam cleaning. Between them, Scott, Laurie, Lucy and the Revills had found the connection between the first two victims. It was Darwin's urine. They had probably found the source of the infection.

Laurie looked at the beagle and then at Megan. "I'll need to test if he's the source. I want blood first. I can take a sample right now."

"No," Megan cried. "It can't be. It can't have come from us!"

"That's why I need the blood. Then I can find out for certain." As calmly as possible, Laurie added, "And I have to organize someone to muzzle him and take him away. Then we can test his urine and excrement as well – in safety."

"No!"

"Yes," Laurie responded firmly. "To tell you the truth, I'm terrified right now, being here in the same room with him. Remember, we haven't got a cure. If any of us pick up the virus from him, we might as well sign the death certificate right here and now. For your own sakes, for Justin's, you've got to let us take him away."

"What'll happen if he *is* carrying the disease?" Barry asked.

Laurie took a deep breath. "I'm sorry. If he's the source, we'll have to put him down and incinerate his body. There's no place for sentimentality here. He's obviously docile but he has the capacity to kill a large number of people in the most unimaginable way. We'd take tissue samples for study and then we'd have to destroy every last molecule of him."

By phone, Laurie requested CDSC chemists to disinfect the Revill's house and garden – and everywhere else that the Revills could remember taking their dog. She also arranged for animal handlers to collect Darwin immediately. She decided to take a blood sample only when the dog could be handled safely in the Biolevel 4 unit. She would not risk frightening him in case he contaminated his home with urine or faeces again.

Walking back to their own house, Laurie put her hand on her son's shoulder and said, "Well spotted, Scott. You should be proud. A lot of lives are going to be saved because you saw the Bolivian connection." She slapped him on the back.

Immediately, Scott fell to the ground with a groan.

Chapter 19

Darryl announced to his assembled colleagues, "Priority one complete. We got the source. It's confirmed as the dog imported from Bolivia. His blood and excrement are absolutely riddled with the virus. So, we owe a big big thank you to an astute Scott Henman who cracked the Bolivian connection, to his friends and mum who twigged the link between the beagle and our first two casualties."

The team let out a spontaneous cheer but Darryl did not allow any feelings of triumph to last long.

"I think we can see how this epidemic happened," he continued. "It was nothing to do with the outbreak in Zaire – a different haemorrhagic fever altogether. In Bolivia this dog harboured Machupo haemorrhagic fever. Inside him, the virus mutated into a slightly modified form. That's evolution in a creature called Darwin, would you believe? Anyway, brought to England, the new strain found itself dumped on a Tinkers Bridge pavement where it attracted the local flies and gnats. They walked all over it. The gnats were the ones that provided the cosiest home for the virus. It multiplied inside the insects and, whenever a carrier gnat nibbled a human being, the virus got injected. The two exceptions were Oliver Church and Tammy Smith – the vital first casualties. Oliver got it directly from the dog's faeces on the owners' carpet and Tammy picked it up direct from Darwin's performance in the animal centre." Darryl paused before adding, "And, if you're worrying about Darwin's quarantine kennel, I've already called them. Because they're dealing with potentially diseased dogs, they're very careful with hygiene. No workers come into direct contact with the animals' excrement. It all gets thoroughly disinfected. They're in the clear."

One of Darryl's CDSC colleagues said, "To be honest, I'm more worried about other dogs in this area."

"I know," Darryl responded. "Darwin could've infected them. Transmission's likely when they smell his urine or faeces. So, we're going to cull all pet dogs inside the barrier. I'll give the order. Obviously, I'm not in this job to make myself popular." Darryl sighed and said, "Now, to end any speculation I have to report that, yes, Scott Henman is in for observation. Laurie's not here because she's running tests on his blood. I can't think of a worse job to give a mother. I really can't." He shook his head and then prompted, "Heather?"

Heather Caldbeck had requested the uncomfortable job of nursing Scott. She reported, "He's putting up a good fight against the flu-like stage but he's poorly. We can't be sure he's got the virus because he hasn't progressed to the bleeding phase but he reckons he was bitten by a gnat eight days ago. He didn't think anything more about it – it was before we knew the carrier. But the bad news is that Darwin was around at the time and he'd just done his business on the pavement. It could well have been a contaminated gnat." She couldn't bring herself to announce the obvious and awful conclusion. Her worries about bringing in the virus from Zaire had been replaced by anxiety for Scott.

"Eight days," Darryl stressed. "He's right on schedule for the flu-like stage." Darryl paused and then said, "Do what you can for him, Heather. I'd rather we didn't have to lose the hero of the hour. Right. Let's crack on for Scott's sake, for those we've got in Isolation already, and for all those who'll come to us in the next eight days. All effort goes into Priority two: treating the victims and finding a cure."

At the university, Laurie almost shouted at the CDSC team leader, "I did the tests, Darryl. I did them twice to make sure. Scott's infected! His blood's seething."

Darryl put his hand on her shoulder but there was no comfort that he could offer. He murmured, "He's a day into the tough flu symptoms."

"We've got three days to come up with a cure. Three days!"

He nodded. "Another day of worsening flu-type problems and then two days of. . ." He looked into Laurie's face.

"Torture," she said to finish his sentence. Laurie was strong but she was also deeply emotional. Tears formed in her eyes. "I can't let him die, Darryl," she exclaimed. "He's only had a quarter – a fifth – of a life. I haven't taken him to see the pyramids, the Grand Canyon, not even Devon. I was too wrapped up. . ."

"Laurie, all your work so far has been for this moment. We're in a strong position to attack it."

"He doesn't deserve. . ."

Darryl interrupted. "No, he doesn't. Neither does anyone else. That's why I'm going to be a cold-hearted bully. That's why I want you to pull yourself together and get stuck in. You're a professional. Don't let them all down now, Laurie."

"Oh, yeah. We're going to develop a cure in three days," she said desperately. "It's like colds and AIDS. People have struggled for years to cure viral infections and we're going to do it in three days?"

"Exactly. Come on. Let's get into the lab. Discussing it here in the corridor isn't going to help. I'll give you a hand. You never know what we might turn up. Scott's in good hands – Heather's looking after him – so your best bet's to stay here and work with me like you've never worked before. Agreed?"

Laurie hesitated, wiped her eyes and then nodded. "OK, I'll try. But how do we start? What do we do?"

"First, I'm going to e-mail every pharmaceutical company in Britain, asking them for samples of every antiviral drug that's still at the experimental stage."

"Will they co-operate?"

Darryl nodded firmly. "To get their drugs tested for free against a brand new virus? To get enormous publicity if one of them works? They'll have them here before lunch."

At the entrance to the hospital, Lucy exploded. "What do you mean, we're not allowed in?"

"No visitors," the security officer stated bluntly.

"Do you know who we are?" she uttered, trying her luck.

Being friends of Scott Henman and contributing to the discovery of the source of the outbreak, however, did not give them a passport to the wards. "Yeah. I know who you are. You're visitors. And visitors aren't allowed."

Inside the building, Scott was feeling lousy. He had a fever, shaking with cold while in fact his body baked. He hadn't managed to eat any food because he felt nauseous and he'd vomited several times.

Heather had moved him to Isolation once his mother had completed her tests. He wasn't yet showing outward signs of haemorrhagic fever but it was only a matter of time. Fearfully, Heather monitored the colour of his eyes. "How you doing, Scott?" she asked sympathetically.

Scott let out a weary breath. "I know a body's just a collection of slimy tubes and giblets wrapped in meat and hung on bones. It's just that I've never felt like it till now."

"I think we're a lot more than that," Heather responded automatically.

Scott did not reply to her comment. He said, "I always thought action was what happened to everyone else, never to me. Girlfriends, booze, all-night parties, naughty substances, getting into trouble. All those things I'm supposed to get involved in, because I'm a seventeen-year-old, they all happened somewhere else, to someone else. Now I'm getting a piece of the action. And it's not a lot of fun."

Heather smiled at him. She wished that the

whites of his eyes would stay that way for ever. "Your mum sends her love. She can't be here much because she's working on a cure. She'd like to be with you but she's got to get on in the lab if she's going to help you."

Scott nodded and winced. "I understand."

Outside the hospital, Syreeta watched, waited, listened. She still tailed ambulances, other vehicles and people, scavenging stories that would enhance her portfolio of articles.

Laurie and Darryl were studying hastily drawn schematics of how antibodies interact with infected cells when Colin put his head round the door. The technician said, "You've got visitors."

"Visitors?"

"Justin Revill and Lucy Metcalfe. They say you know them."

Laurie replied, "OK. Tell them we're busy but bring them in for a minute or two."

It was Lucy who took the lead. "We went to see Scott but they wouldn't let us in," she explained. "That's not nice. It must be rotten for him in there. We think he deserves visitors."

Darryl looked at Laurie and then replied,

"So do we. Can you go straight back?"

"To the hospital? Yes."

He glanced at his watch and said, "In exactly an hour I'll have a nurse called Heather Caldbeck at the entrance. I'll sort it out from here by phone. She'll get you in. But you'll have to understand, you won't be able to sit on his bed and chat. We've got to keep you safe. You'll be on the other side of some glass and you'll only be able to talk through a phone thing."

"Better than nothing," Lucy said.

Softly, Laurie added, "Tell him I'm thinking of him. But I can only help him by staying here."

On the path back to Passmore, a friendly woman struck up a conversation with Rev and Lucy. After she'd made the obligatory comments on the hot weather and the epidemic, she said, "I couldn't help noticing you came out of Dr Henman's department. She must be a brave woman. Do you know her, and if she's making any headway against this horrible disease?"

Lucy eyed the newcomer and refused to answer but Rev saw no harm in her. In the face of the common enemy – haemorrhagic fever – all humans had become sociable. "It's all a bit beyond me but, yes, she's found the source and taken it out," he said without mentioning his own involvement. "There shouldn't be any new infections. Now, she's got a way of seeing the virus. With Professor Wheeler, she's trying to figure out how to cure people who've already got it. She needs to do it quickly."

"Oh? Why do you say that? Any particular reason?" the stranger probed.

Lucy interrupted the exchange, saying, "The quicker they get a cure, obviously the more sick people they'll save."

The woman persisted with her questioning as if she was more than merely neighbourly and curious. "Does she have an infected friend or relative?"

Lucy thought that the woman was becoming intrusive. "Are you a reporter?" she asked.

"I'm just interested. . ."

"Forget it," Lucy said, seeing through the answer straight away. She didn't imagine that Laurie and Scott would fancy having a journalist sniffing around. "I think the phrase is 'No comment'."

* * *

Scott's throat was so sore that swallowing and speaking were incredibly painful. He felt an ominous uncontrollable throbbing behind his eyeballs.

On the internal telephone, Lucy chirped, "You look like something that came out the wrong end of a cow."

Scott found it difficult to turn his head on the pillow. His neck was swollen as if he had tried to swallow a deflated football and it had caught in his throat and now someone was pumping it up mercilessly. The window was a few metres – or several miles, it didn't matter – to his left, but he was pleased to see Rev and Lucy. He was too scared to talk about himself, too scared to be serious. "Well," he said into the microphone above his head, "we're all doomed anyway. A ring of invisible matter is heading towards us from the centre of the galaxy – like a ripple on a pond."

"Oh?"

"Didn't you know?" he said, feigning surprise. "It'll shake up comets around the sun and send them crashing into the Earth. Death to the entire planet. Every single creature."

"Are you making this up?" Rev put in. His

face suggested that he thought his friend was delirious.

"No, I'm not," Scott replied.

"That's not so good. When's this going to happen?"

"Three hundred and fifty million years from today."

Suddenly Rev realized that his mate was joking. "Now you've really got me worried," he said with a strained smile.

"There's worse," Scott continued. He broke off to clear his throat and grimace at the discomfort. "If the dark matter misses us after all, the sun'll bake all the water from the planet anyway. Either way, we've had it."

"And when's that?"

"In three and a half billion years' time."

Rev shook his head and lost his smile. "How are you, Scott? Really."

"Bearing up, I suppose. That means not very well. But it's not just me. There's another seventeen people in here, all trying to go up the down escalator. They're all falling further behind than me. Well, there was seventeen at the last count. It could be sixteen, fifteen or fourteen by now. And there'll be more – people who got bitten by carrier gnats before they got sprayed out of existence, or who came into contact with Darwin's mess." Scott asked, "Are you two OK?"

They both nodded. "No symptoms yet."

"Your mum?"

Rev said, "Mum? She's . . . like a zombie. Broken. You see, her whole world order's collapsed. It used to be nice and neat. Us clean middle-class people were the goodies and the people in Tinkers Bridge and Netherfield were the baddies. All the nastiness and crime was the fault of the baddies. Simple. Now, she knows the nastiest nastiness came from Passmore – from her own house – not Tinkers Bridge. Her world's turned upside down. And she blames herself for the virus. It's a tough thing to live with."

"But it's not terminal." There was an implication in his croaky tone that really she was one of the lucky ones.

"*Your* mum's still hard at it," Rev replied. "She's trying to find a cure, Scott."

"She's thinking of you," Lucy put in. "She asked us to say."

Scott nodded faintly.

"You'll be all right, Scott. I'm sure," Lucy said in a voice that quavered slightly.

Scott smiled wrily. "Believe me, when this bug bites, you stay bit."

On the way down the long white depressing corridor back to the normal world, Rev suddenly halted. Trying not to show his emotion, he looked at Lucy and said, "I can't imagine a life without Scott."

Lucy nodded and held his arm. The disease had finally subdued her.

Chapter 20

UNDERGRADUATE NOTES: MODULE 4; ANTIBODIES. L. HENMAN.

During two billion years, our immune systems have evolved into a complicated means of defence but they are not perfect. Some types of white blood cell roam the body, destroying any bacteria and viruses that they recognize as foreign. A different type does not target free-swimming microbes but attacks human cells that have gone bad (e.g. cancerous cells and cells that contain viruses). Antibodies are proteins that are churned out by yet another class of white blood cells: the lymphocytes. Antibodies do not hunt down any and every threat. They are released to counteract one specific threat. An antibody for measles combats only the measles virus and an invasion of the measles virus turns on only measles antibodies. To be able to do this, the immune system must have encountered that particular virus previously. Lymphocytes also make killer T cells which scavenge for body cells that harbour viruses and puncture them. The corrupt cells release their contents so that the freed viruses are exposed to the powerful antibodies and white blood cells that can destroy them.

Like the viruses themselves, our antibodies mutate. Hence, new and different antibodies are being made continually by the lymphocytes in a hit-and-miss fashion. These new antibodies are used against invasions of new viruses. That is biology's defence against fresh challenges to the body. Sooner or later, a human being will produce an effective antibody for a new infection. Problems: (a) it may be produced later rather than sooner, and (b) harmful bacteria and viruses mutate into new forms much faster than the antibodies of the animals that they infect.

After setting up more experiments with mice, and purging herself in the decontamination zone, Laurie was a brighter pink than ever before. To keep her going, Darryl handed her a strong coffee sweetened with sugar. He sat her down at a desk and said, "Here's the problem. Antibodies haven't seen the virus before and they can't recognize it. Besides, once it's inside body cells, it's disguised – protected by wrapping itself in a body cell. So far, no victim's hit it lucky and evolved a defence against it. First theory: maybe the killer T cells can't recognize an infected cell when they see one. But maybe they can. Second theory: maybe they grab a bad cell but can't puncture it. Or, third theory, perhaps they puncture it but don't summon the immune system to come and attack the released virus."

Dejected, Laurie replied, "If you really put your mind to it, you can probably come up with another ten theories." She looked at the computer terminal, buzzing with micrographs of the relentless killing machine. "Seen anything?"

Darryl rubbed his strained eyes. "Not yet."

"I want to do some experiments with monkeys," Laurie announced.

"Monkeys?"

"Mice are OK but they're not good models for human beings. Monkeys are a lot closer. I'm going to give them the virus and see if we get any immune responses that'll mimic what we want in people."

Darryl frowned. "It's dangerous. Handling infected monkeys will be a lot trickier than handling mice safely. They'll struggle. If they scratch, bite, smash a syringe, anything, you're infected."

"I know," Laurie replied. "But it's not your son who's got the damn disease, is it?" She stormed away to speak to Colin about getting a supply of monkeys into the BL4 secure laboratory.

Chapter 21

Dressed in her faithful low-cut blouse, Syreeta tried her luck with certain types of young men and sad middle-aged men in The Moorings. She flitted round the pub, a cheery word here and there, seeking easy prey. She was sampling men like a bee samples flowers. Intuition drew her towards a young man drinking alone at the bar. She talked to him about the plague, the inconvenience of living in a restricted area, the eradication of the gnats. And he bought her a drink.

"Why are all the dogs being rounded up, do you think?" she enquired.

"S'obvious," he told her. "Chap next door to me would rather they took 'is wife than 'is dog." He laughed aloud.

"Why are they taking the dogs, then?" Syreeta pressed.

He gave a shrug that suggested he knew but he wondered what was in it for him to let on. "I haven't seen you in here before. . ."

Syreeta gave a coy smile. "You weren't going to say, 'Do you come here often?' were you?" Ignoring the opportunity to tell him that she was a reporter, she edged tantalizingly close to him so that her bare arm touched his.

"Well," he answered, believing that he'd worked out what was on offer, "we reckon it's the dogs what's giving us this plague."

"All the dogs wouldn't suddenly get infected," Syreeta replied. "Would they?"

"S'obvious," he repeated. "One dog got it, the others got it from him by doin' what dogs do. Shovin' their noses. . ."

"That's really interesting," Syreeta butted in eagerly. "Do you know whose dog had it in the first place?"

"Well, there's a rumour. Mate o' mine saw them taking away a dog this morning. Muzzled and stuff. All in fancy gear – the men, not the dog." He laughed again.

"Where from?"

Taking his time, the man blew smoke from

his cigarette and created a cloud around the two of them. Syreeta hated the smell and wanted to turn away but she forced herself to smile at him instead.

"It was in Passmore," he said eventually.

"Fancy. A Passmore place." She shook her head in feigned surprise. "Do you want another?" She pointed to his empty glass. After she'd got him a beer, she asked, "Which number was the house in Passmore, then? Do you know? Just out of interest."

"Not sure if I should tell you that," he said with a playful grin.

"No harm in it," Syreeta said with a dismissive wave of her hand. She undid the top button of her blouse and pulled the material away from her skin, saying, "Phew, it's hot in here, isn't it?"

He lifted his hungry eyes back to her face but he didn't seem interested in the weather. He could say only, "Mmm." He was totally captivated by her.

Syreeta shook her long hair behind her shoulders and asked again, "Which house did you say it was?"

Doug turned the lights off and cruised down

the last part of Newport Road in the dark. There was just enough light from the occasional street lamp and the string of yellow lights on the raised and heavily defended H7 road to guide him to the tiny roundabout and car park where the road came to an abrupt end. He got out of his small van, closed the door with barely a sound, and walked along the footpath towards the forbidden area. There was a high hedge on his right, shielding him from view of the houses. On his left, the sheep in Ouzel Valley Park shifted restlessly. In one hand, he carried his bag of tools. He peered at his watch, wondering if his brother had already taken up position on the other side of the bundle of razor wire that barricaded the underpass. Les should have easily evaded the attention of the patrolling troops. On the other side of H7, there was only the park, sheep and plenty of tree cover. More like quiet countryside than a town and nothing at all like the concrete image of Milton Keynes.

Les had arranged it all by phone. By now, nearly two a.m., he should have left his house by St Mary's in Woughton-on-the-Green. He should have taken the footpath behind the church into the park, walked past the site of the medieval village, and made for the shrouded subway under H7.

Doug froze for a minute while an army jeep stopped above him. Two soldiers got out of the khaki vehicle and, after an exchange and some loud laughing, two others climbed inside. It seemed to be a change of shift. Doug muffled a sneeze with his free hand. He waited for the soldiers to stroll away from the immediate area of the underpass and then, unseen, crept up to it. He did not expect to be spotted. After all, the patrols were looking out for people and animals on the other side of the road breaking out from the quarantine zone. The walkway seemed to disappear into a black hole where it tunnelled under Chaffron Way. In the shadow of the street lamps, Doug's eyes took a long while to adjust. He walked into the concrete cavern, squatted down by the barbed wire, unzipped his bag and extracted his garden gloves and wire cutters. The job shouldn't take long. He didn't have to make a large hole.

Alert and curious, the toy dog stood beside Les. The Pomeranian's coat was long and coarse. Frequent grooming had made it particularly fluffy around the neck, legs and tail where its hair was almost white. The coat on the rest of its body and its fox-like face was dark brown. The dog's dark eyes bulged out, its tiny ears were erect and its tail was tightly curled over its back. Les stroked his prize pet so that it wouldn't get nervous and issue one of its sharp yaps.

There were no soldiers in view. Les took a deep breath and left the generous cover of the bushes and trees at the edge the footpath. He dashed silently up to the closed underpass. Beside him, the spoiled Pomeranian was only fifteen centimetres tall but it strutted forward showily and smugly like a supermodel. Les felt vulnerable in the open but someone on H7 would have to lean right over the rail of the bridge to see him below. Even so, he recalled all those rumours about the army shooting someone who had tried to escape. Trying to dispel his misgivings, he concentrated on the job in hand. Listening carefully, he heard the characteristic clicking of cutters biting through thick wire. Doug had always been a reliable brother, a professional tradesman, a helping hand out of a quagmire. Les called out softly, "Is that you, Doug?"

"Yeah," said the subdued voice on the other side of the barbed wire.

"It's happening like I said," Les complained in a whisper. "They're collecting up every dog in the neighbourhood. It's a cull. But I tell you, they're not getting their hands on Christie here. He's far too precious. A double champion."

Slightly wearied, Doug replied, "I know, Les. But don't get hot under the collar about it now. Keep your voice down." There was another snip and a small piece of the wire came away. Stifling another sneeze, Doug murmured, "Soon be there."

"Another summer cold?" Les asked.

"As always," Doug grumbled.

Two anxious minutes later, Les saw his brother's gloved hand. The sudden movement looked like a nervous rabbit in the dark entrance to a warren. "You're through," Les breathed.

"Is it big enough?"

Les got down on his elbows and peered into the hole. Christie's immaculate coat might brush against some of the loose ends but he wouldn't get caught on the spiky bits. "Just," he said into the void. He ushered the

Pomeranian towards the gap but it was like asking royalty, complete with finery, to go down into a coal mine. King Christopher Diamond of Lilliput refused. Les muttered, "You'll have to call him, Doug. He knows your voice well enough."

The dog with the exotic show-name listened to Doug's familiar whisper, sniffed at the gap in the barricade and then looked quizzically at Les.

Les nodded. "Go to Doug. Go find him." Gently, he pushed the pompous dog by its dainty backside.

Christie got the idea. He didn't want to leave his owner but he sensed that it was important to follow Doug's scent. He pranced into the strange burrow.

"Got him?" Les asked apprehensively.

"Yes. No problem."

"Is he OK? Not damaged."

"He's fine, Les. Stop worrying."

"All right. I'll collect him when this thing's over. Now, remember, you've got to brush him every—"

"Yes, yes," Doug interrupted. "Tell me by phone, if you must. Let's get out of here."

Les crept away from the subway, glancing

back to the bright lights on Chaffron Way. With razor wire and troops, it looked like the perimeter of a secret Government establishment. Then he set off for home.

At once, someone barked at him. "You! What are you doing?"

Les turned and found himself squinting into a harsh beam that came from the main road. He could just make out a tall figure beside the spotlight. Using the routine he'd rehearsed in his head, he staggered, nearly fell and shouted back, "You what?"

The soldier repeated, "What are you up to?"

Les turned aside, leaned over a bush and pretended to be sick with loud accompanying noises. He needed to give Doug and Christie enough time to get away without being seen.

Up on the embankment, the soldier's tone changed. "Are you OK?" he shouted.

Les replied in a slurred voice. "I just . . . I've had one or two. You don't know what it's like in here. You've got to have a drink. The bugs don't get you when you've had a few. The alcohol keeps 'em away." He waved an arm loosely as if he was not in total command of his movements. Then he tottered again.

Now mildly amused, the soldier called, "Do

you want me to call the police to escort you home?"

"Police? If you like but, no, I'm all right. I'm a bit off course but I know this place. Got my bearings now. I'm on my way. That way." He pointed vaguely behind himself.

"Good. Home's the best place for you."

While Les meandered away, occasionally stumbling for effect, the shaft of light followed him until the curve of the tree-lined path excluded it.

Chapter 22

By morning, Scott's throat had become so sore that he could not swallow at all. He was fed by intravenous drip. His eyes were distinctly bloodshot and his skin showed red rashes. He rolled around on the bed, contorting his body into unnatural shapes, tangling with the plastic tubes. Heather knew exactly what it meant. Blood was clotting in his capillaries. His liver, kidneys and spleen were choking on solid clumps of coagulated blood and tissue. His urine was tinged with faint red. It meant that he was deteriorating along with everyone else who had unintentionally provided a habitat for the grotesque virus.

Heather passed her gloved hand across the young man's moist brow and smiled at him.

Scott recognized her smile. The worst sort of smile. It was suffused with helpless pity. The nurse must have been about thirty. Short dark hair. Very attractive. Despite her years, her face showed no sign of ageing. She had the soft smooth skin of a teenager. The gown that she wore left only hints of her figure but Scott's imagination filled in the rest. He saw a breathtaking shape. Then he turned away so that he would not torment himself with ideas well beyond his reach, with things that the virus would never let him experience. Next to him, Heather was a light year away. She belonged to a race that did not have the plague. He belonged to a different race altogether. She was beautiful and he was an ugly squirming mess. He was seventeen and she was much older. And she pitied him.

Scott's head filled with unwelcome thoughts like the unwanted chords of a catchy song. Everything that the virus would deny him played on his brain. A career, his chance for fame and glory and riches, a car, independence, a woman, love and sex. A future. To himself he muttered, "All that school work and sex education for nothing."

When he heard a quiet giggle, he turned his

heavy head back towards Heather. Her smile had changed. It was now just natural and warm and friendly, even appreciative. Mixed with an inevitable trace of sympathy. After all, she was a nurse. "I've got a shock for you. You never finish learning, Scott. Sickness always strikes just after you've learned something but never tried it out." Heather said it awkwardly, not quite knowing how to respond in the circumstances. As a midwife, she was more used to the infinite potential of young lives. She knew much less about dealing with potential lost. "Anyway," she added, "you've got the best brains working away to make sure you get back to school after we've cracked this. Lucky you."

"Can't wait to get back to chemistry homework," he murmured cynically. The sad thing, Scott thought, was that he *was* pining for chemistry homework. He was pining for being normal again. Now, it struck him that an ordinary human life was extraordinary, a miracle. All he wanted was a chance at an ordinary miracle.

Syreeta was intrigued when she recognized the young man who answered the door. It was the lad who, with a tubby girl, had visited Dr Henman at the university. Syreeta had spoken to them on their way back to the hospital and she'd picked up a hint that Dr Henman had an infected relative there. Syreeta had already done her research on the biologist. There was no evidence of a partner, only a son called Scott. It had to be him. So, Syreeta guessed, this lad in the doorway was a friend of Scott Henman and now it seemed that his dog may have been responsible for spreading the disease. Life had an odd way of coming up with ironies. The journalist's imagination went into overdrive. She felt a sensational exclusive coming on.

She had it in mind to take the part of a vet or police officer but she decided to play it straight after all. Besides, the boy's girlfriend had already guessed that she was a reporter. She would have to wheedle her way in without subterfuge this time. "I'm doing a story for a newspaper," she announced, "on these poor dogs who've been put down."

Rev picked up a note from the telephone table in the hall and said, "I'd have thought you'd get all you want from this."

Syreeta narrowed her eyes as she read the

first few sentences. It was an explanation put out by Professor Wheeler and the hospital authorities.

"Delivered this morning," Rev told her.

"I haven't got mine yet," Syreeta replied. "But I'm more interested in the human stories behind it. Pensioners left alone because their pet's been taken away and destroyed. . ."

"We don't exactly come into that category," Rev retorted.

"But your dog has been taken away?"

"Yes." Rev saw no harm in confirming it.

"I bet you have a story, then. Everyone has. How do you feel about losing your dog? How are your mum and dad taking it? Who do you blame for it? Do you really think it was necessary?"

Rev spoke through a slowly narrowing gap. "I don't think we want to be in the papers about that."

The door was closing on her scoop. Syreeta decided to go for the throat. "Is it true what they're saying – that your dog was the one who had the virus?"

Rev answered with body language. His shocked face said it all and he hesitated before slamming the door shut.

Syreeta smiled slyly. She'd got an answer. She'd found out who had inflicted a plague on Milton Keynes. Time to interview the neighbours about the Revills and the hospital staff about Scott Henman. She needed to squeeze out the basic facts. For the rest she could extrapolate, speculate or invent.

Inside the house, Rev went back to the lounge where Ross McGavin was trying to comfort his mother.

Darryl kept his bleary eyes on the screen while he answered the phone so that he did not have to interrupt his work. Some army officer reported in his ear that the barricade at a subway under H7 had been breached during the night. "What?" Darryl exclaimed.

"We found a hole made with wire cutters."

Darryl cursed loudly and with venom. "Big enough for a person to get through?"

"No. More like cat size."

"Get the police to throw everything they've got at it," Darryl said urgently. "My bet's on a small dog. Someone didn't want their pet to go up in smoke for the sake of the community and arranged for it to get smuggled out. If it was carrying the virus. . ." He ran out of words. He didn't want to contemplate the repercussions. "I want that dog back in the area and in the lab for tests. Everyone who came into contact with it goes into Observation for eight days, minimum." Before he rang off, he added sternly, "And I want its owner's head on a plate."

Inside the Biolevel 4 unit, the virus was killing Laurie's monkeys as effectively as it killed humans. It also ignored every experimental drug that they threw at it.

The work at the hospital's microbiology unit continued. Using the procedure that had become known as the Henman Test, the technicians were clearing the backlog of samples and checking new ones for signs of the virus. Mercifully few contained the deadly microbe.

Gnats: no samples available
*House flies: few samples available; all
    negative*
Other insects: negative
*Bats traced to canal/H9 intersection: droppings
    positive; area being disinfected*
Dogs: all destroyed; four positive

Human contacts with source dog:
Megan Revill: negative
Barry Revill: negative
Justin Revill: negative
Lucy Metcalfe: sample awaited
Human contacts with other infected dogs:
  three positive
Hospital/research staff:
  Darryl Wheeler: negative
  Heather Caldbeck: negative
  Laurie Henman: negative
  Microbiology technicians: all negative
  CDSC team: still monitoring; negative thus
  far

Taking a blood sample from Scott no longer required a hypodermic syringe. His clotting factors exhausted, the crimson fluid was beginning to gush uncontrolled from every orifice, taking the remnants of damaged body tissues with it.

Red and white blood cells were leaking at an alarming rate from his cardiovascular system and into his urine. The white blood cells weren't doing a lot of good. They had already been overwhelmed by the virus, multiplying like crazy, making billions of copies of itself, transforming his body into a virus cloning factory. His insides had become no more than a hatchery. His blood carried jostling viruses to every part of his writhing body. His lungs, stomach, intestine, brain, eyes became filled with the contaminated fluid. His reddened skin was beginning to balloon with the pressure of torrential blood.

Heather warned Rev and Lucy that they weren't going to like what they saw. They weren't going to believe what a virus had done to their friend. "Are you sure you still want to see him?"

Lucy nodded firmly. In a lukewarm voice, Rev said, "Yes." He meant no, of course. He wanted to remember Scott as a healthy young man. But duty – and Lucy – required him to say goodbye to his best mate.

Yet when they saw him through the glass, they both gulped, unable to speak.

With superhuman effort, Scott turned towards them. He swallowed the foul blood that was leaking from his gums and forced words past his bloated throat. "Sorry. I must look a sight."

Lucy reacted first. "Oh, Scott. Don't. . ."

"It's a bit more than a nosebleed."

Rev almost shouted at him. "Don't you give in to it."

"My body doesn't really belong to me any more," Scott croaked. "It belongs to the virus. It's their home now."

Rev could not take it. He put his hands to his face and flew back down the corridor.

Lucy managed to stay at the window for a little longer. Trying to smile and crack a joke, she said, "You're losing your hair, old man." But the quip didn't work. She felt awkward and guilty for making it. Quickly, she added, "It's real trendy to take it all off." Tongue-tied, she gave up. There was nothing meaningful she could say in the face of this awful disease. "All the best, Scott. We'll be thinking of you." Like Rev, Lucy hurried away.

Fighting back the tears, Heather changed Scott's drip and said a few useless words. She had seen it all before, of course. Far too many times. The young, the old. She'd watched them all come and go. After two to four days, each one was sealed in a box and wheeled away by the porters. The victims would be embraced only by flames. Until now, Heather had coped with it all. She tried hard to take it all in her stride – but Dr Henman's son. . . It seemed that the vindictive virus was retaliating against the person who had discovered its hiding-place and the woman whose work threatened to defeat it.

When Darryl darted across from the university to catch up on news and to collect Scott's latest samples, Heather crashed into him. She couldn't help it. She sobbed on his shoulder.

Darryl didn't have to ask what was the matter. He knew the almost intolerable pressure of watching helplessly as one patient after another was wheeled in, and wheeled out to the incinerator. Letting her weep the frustration out of her system, he whispered, "You're doing a terrific job, Heather. But take a break. You've got to think of yourself as well as the sick."

She sobbed, "It's nothing but a vicious, sub-microscopic thug."

"Yes." Darryl had grown fond of this woman who had volunteered to help the team – even though it was an unspeakably risky task well outside her normal duties – and volunteered to share her house with him. When she lifted her head off his shoulder and looked into his face, he was tempted to kiss her. But he could not defy his own rules. He might have been contaminated since his last blood test and, if so, a kiss would be enough to spread it to Heather.

Heather realized what was in his mind. And she knew why he stopped himself. She shook her head and said, "Sorry."

"What for?" he asked.

She uncoupled herself. "I should be more professional."

Darryl put a hand to his itchy neck and scratched at two days' craggy stubble. He must look rough, he realized, but recently his appearance had been the last thing on his mind. "Heather," he replied sincerely, "I've never met anyone more professional, more caring, than you. If it didn't get to you sometimes, you wouldn't be human. If it didn't get to you, you wouldn't be any good at what you're doing. You're working miracles."

Heather shook her head. "No. If I could work miracles, I'd have saved someone by now. That's the only miracle that matters."

"You want to be relieved? I could draft in someone else."

She wiped her eyes and nose. "No. Let me down a stiff drink. Then I'll be OK."

Darryl nodded. "How's Scott?"

"He's one brave lad. He's fighting. At the stage he's at, no one else has managed to say a word. He's still struggling to communicate." She paused and said, "Darryl?"

"What?"

"You ought to send Laurie over. No matter how important her work is. I don't know how much longer he'll be able to communicate. Not long. Laurie'll want to speak to him."

"You think she should say goodbye."

Heather's eyes said yes.

"I'll make sure she's here," Darryl said, "but not to say goodbye. I won't have anyone saying that till I'm sure we've failed to crack it and he's about to be pronounced dead."

Heather touched his arm, almost turning him round. "Go and get on with it, then. You won't crack it standing here talking to me."

"Are you going to be OK?"

Heather managed a smile. "Shift yourself. I've got patients waiting for me."

Chapter 23

Laurie was hopelessly torn. The only way to save her son was to continue the research effort. But her place was beside him. Yet, beside him, she couldn't do anything for him. She couldn't even touch him with a bare hand. She couldn't even kiss him without a piece of material intervening. Besides, it would only hurt him. She might as well go back to the lab. But the feverish investigations looked bleak. The fatigued scientists could not see where the breakthrough was going to come from – or if it was going to come at all. So, she might as well stay with Scott. But. . .

Whichever way she turned, a voice in her head objected, "But. . ."

Scott squirmed on the bed, leaving behind

the linen. Much of his hair was scattered across his pillow. He was virtually bald. He opened his eyes and, for an instant, they shone. "Mum."

Laurie nodded, trying not to show her shock and torment. "Yes, it's me."

"Are *you* still OK?" he enquired. There was a gap of about a second between each word. It was the time he needed to steel himself for the effort.

Laurie was taken aback. She barely recognized her own son's voice. It came out as something between a growl, a whisper and a gurgle. "Don't worry about me. The virus is easier to control in a lab. It was at its most dangerous when it was hiding somewhere in the neighbourhood." The germ, and the fact that she'd handled infected animals, still scared her silly but she wasn't going to admit it to Scott. Now, she wished she could hug an infected human. She looked away for a moment and then turned back to him. "It's you I'm worried about. You know, I can hardly remember you ever being really ill. You were lucky. When all your mates got chickenpox, asthma, broken arms and legs, you got a twenty-four-hour cold. I'm not sure how to deal with this, Scott. I'm not used to it."

"Nor me."

Suddenly, it occurred to Laurie that she ought to get in touch with Scott's father. He had a right to know. But he'd shown no interest for years. Perhaps that disqualified him. Laurie decided not to go through the pain of communicating with him unless Scott asked for him.

Scott's eyes were dull red again. "You've given up on me, though."

"What?" she exclaimed. "Never. Why do you say that?" Gloved, she mopped the streaky red liquid coming from the corner of his left eye.

"Because you're here," he said, wincing with the pain of contact.

He was right, of course. She thought it was hopeless. But she would never say so to Scott. She would push herself to work harder, believing it was hopeless, but refusing to give in. "I just couldn't bear to carry on without seeing you," she said. "That's all. I want to be here with you and I have to be somewhere else. Do you understand?"

Even through clouded eyes, Scott saw past his mum's words. "It's almost impossible to win the National Lottery," he struggled to say, "but people still buy tickets."

Laurie nodded. "OK. I'll go back to work and carry on looking for the right combination, looking for your lucky numbers."

"Mum?"

"Yes?"

"You don't need to get Dad," Scott stuttered. "You're all I've needed."

Laurie felt her lower lip beginning to quiver. She smiled and replied, "Don't *you* give up after lecturing me about it. See you later, Scott."

Back in front of the images from the electron microscope, Darryl suddenly let out a cry. "At last!"

"What is it?" Laurie queried, dashing up to him.

Darryl tapped the screen. As usual, it was filled with depressing pictures of cells invaded by worm-like viruses. But one out of hundreds was different. A white blood cell was attached to it. The two arms of a killer T cell gripped it like a small boy clutching a giant beach-ball.

"No antibodies attacking the virus," Darryl remarked, "but a killer T's recognized a contaminated body cell."

"Which sample is this?"

Darryl cast a glance at Laurie and nodded. "It's the one you want it to be, Laurie. It's one of Scott's." He paused and then drove home the good news again. "His immune system's managed to recognize a corrupt cell."

Laurie's half-smile was also half-grimace. She muttered, "The cell's not affected, though. Look. It's not been punctured or attacked. The virus is carrying on regardless."

"True. But attaching a T cell's the first step," Darryl said optimistically. He stood up, ready for action. "Right. I want all his samples. And I want more samples from him. I'm going to isolate these killer Ts."

"Why? They're not doing any good."

"Because I want to try grafting something on to the end of them. You see, this killer T's doing a great job but it's only half a job. It's engaged the enemy at one end but it's not calling the immune system to send more front-line troops to attack the cell it's got hold of. If I could graft on to its other end a unit that'll attract white blood cells, they'll flock to the virus and maybe one of them'll be effective against it."

Laurie nodded slowly. "Got you. You want

to create a bridge between the captured cell and the immune system. One end of a modified T cell grabs a diseased cell, the other calls out the defence in force. A mutation might just crack it."

"I'll call Heather to get over here with as much of his blood as she can collect. Are you with me on this? You'll have to work with me in Biolevel 4 and it's all or nothing. There won't be time to look at any other solutions. We follow this lead and drop everything else. If we're barking up the wrong tree, Scott's. . ."

Laurie took a deep breath and then let it go slowly. She forgot all about her tiredness, her pessimism, her embarrassment at going through decontamination and disinfection with a man. "I haven't got a better idea," she said, making for the air locks.

When Heather arrived with the priceless, dangerous blood samples and handed them over to Colin, for a while she watched Laurie and Darryl standing side by side at a fume cupboard. They had their backs to her and were concentrating so hard on their research that they did not notice her behind the thick glass. Really, she wished she could be in there, working beside Darryl, but she was just a midwife who found herself in the role of nurse. She could tend to Scott but she couldn't cure him. Of course, she also had a second reason for feeling a twinge of envy.

Heather jumped when a nearby phone squawked. She recognized it as Darryl's. He had discarded it because he couldn't use it inside the protective clothing and he wouldn't want distractions anyway. She answered the call. "Yes?"

Hesitantly, a child's voice said, "Is that Mummy?" He sounded cheerful at the prospect.

"Er . . . no. I think you must have the wrong. . . Who are you wanting to speak to?"

"Daddy."

"Are you Mark Wheeler?"

"Yes."

"Ah. Then your daddy *is* here. I'm looking at him now, Mark. He's fine but I can't get him for you."

"Why not?"

"He'd want to speak to you but he's doing some very important work. He's trying to make another boy – a bit older than you – well again."

"Is the boy sick?"

"Very sick."

"My daddy's good at making people better."

"He's *very* good at it." Heather asked, "Did you want to say anything to your dad? I can tell him later or get him to call you."

"When's he coming back?"

"Well, I don't know, Mark. It shouldn't be too long but it'll be a few days, I'm afraid. But he's thinking of you all the time. That I do know."

The young boy let out an almost adult sigh. "I wish we were going home now."

"He'll be home as soon as he can," Heather said. Remembering the look on Darryl's face when he showed her his son's photograph, she added, "He's very proud of you."

"I hope he fixes the sick boy."

"He'll do his best. I'll tell him you called."

"Are you going to be my new mummy?"

Startled, Heather hesitated. She glanced at the back of Darryl's protective suit. "No, Mark. I'm just your daddy's . . . friend." She could have said colleague but she decided on friend.

"It's good to have a friend," Mark replied, clearly repeating what he had heard some adult say.

Then he was gone. And Heather felt strangely empty.

She headed back to the hospital to fill the emptiness with the needs of patients.

Once the doctor had taken down all of the teenager's details and sent her to Observation, she turned to the girl's parents and said, "As far as you know, was Charlotte bitten by a gnat in the last week?"

At once, both of them replied, "Yes."

The doctor raised her eyebrows. She had never witnessed such a firm answer. Usually, the relatives weren't sure. Either they didn't know or they became vague in the face of distress. The Flynns were different. It seemed to her that they had recited a rehearsed response. She didn't believe them. But why would they lie? She asked, "Has she come into contact with a dog recently? Do you know?"

They seemed confused now, as if they hadn't anticipated the question.

"Do you have a dog?" she enquired.

"We *did*," Les Flynn said, stressing the past tense.

"So, she would've come into contact with

it," the doctor concluded. "What was its name?"

The Flynns glanced at each other. "Why do you want to know that?"

"I've got a list of all the dogs that were destroyed," she replied, "including four that had the virus. If yours was positive, you should have had a blood test by now – just in case – but, in all the confusion, you might've been missed."

Taken by surprise, Les gave the name of the dog across the road. The name of his own dog would not appear on the doctor's list at all. That would create some awkward questions.

After scanning the names, the doctor said, "Well, he was clean, no infection, so either it's a false alarm – hopefully – or we're looking at a gnat bite."

As soon as she left Charlotte's parents, the doctor phoned Security and said, "I've got something funny going on with a chap called Les Flynn. His daughter's probably a victim and he was cagey about questions on sources of infection. Very odd. You might want to check him out. I think you ought to look into his dog."

Chapter 24

Heather stood by the door and breathed in the warm night air. She was troubled. Unless there was a miracle, it would be Scott's last night. He had gone into the motionless stagnant phase that preceded death. The endless sky was clear. An aeroplane's flashing lights drifted across the backdrop of stars. The only sound of traffic was a distant rumble – outside the exclusion zone. In another doorway, a pinpoint of red glowed intermittently. Between the seconds of brightness, it died and fell. One of the hospital staff was taking a crafty outdoor fag.

Heather imagined that she looked a mess. It was only a guess because she had not looked in a mirror for a couple of days. She'd been on her feet for more than twenty-four hours and her muscles ached like crazy. She wondered if Darryl would still take an interest now he'd seen her at her most slovenly. She put her hand to her mouth and coughed.

She could shut out the awesome sky by closing her eyes but she could not escape the awful pictures in her mind, from Yombe's father, Oliver Church and Tammy Smith to Scott Henman. They were the indelible burnt-out wrecks that lay abandoned beside the motorway, crashed out of a rapidly moving world. There was no going back. After the epidemic was over, her life would never be the same. She could not unsee what she had seen. She would need help to deal with the legacy of the virus.

Above her, a steamy cloud billowed from the chimney of the hospital's incinerator.

Rev and Lucy had drunk far too much. Yet alcohol could not wash away the knowledge of what was happening to Scott. And it could not wash away their helplessness. Rev thought that the more he drank, the more he'd deaden the pain. But blissful numbness did not set in. Quite the opposite. Everywhere he looked, he remembered something that he and Scott had done there. Alcohol dissolved the edges of the world and left clear memories of Scott.

On the towpath, Lucy grabbed him abruptly, saying, "If you're not careful, you'll fall in!"

When Rev pointed to the other side of the canal, his arm swayed like a signpost in a gale. "Scott used to claim he pulled a drowning girl out over there. He didn't, of course. It's just that he always wanted to be a hero." Rev chuckled. He watched the distant red glow at the rear of a houseboat moored at the marina, sighed and then added, "Do you know how many A grades he got at GCSE?"

"No."

"Nor me. Too many to count. And he gets on so well with his mum. Sometimes I wish I was him."

Lucy sniffed and wiped an eye. "Not any more."

"No. Not now."

Above Dr Henman, the insistent glow remained green. Whatever she did in the fume cupboard, she was always aware of that green light, always conscious that it could turn red and flash its warning that there was a breach in her protection. A red glow would mean that she was contaminated. A red glow would mean that she was dead.

She'd handled hypodermic syringes and unpredictable, scratching, biting, frightened animals and still the lamp glowed green. The tiniest rupture of her clothing would have changed its colour, would have sent her rushing back into decontamination, to the ultraviolet lights and the painful antiseptic shower. Yet it would have been too late anyway. Once exposed, this virus didn't give second chances.

This night, she was manipulating only test-tubes. Virtually free of hazards. But nothing was totally free of hazards. The tubes contained Scott's infected blood serum. One of them could slip from her weary fingers, smash on the surface and a splinter of broken glass could pierce her suit. A simple accident. That's all it would take to contaminate her, to convert that annoying little light to red. An audible alarm would also sound in her ear. Knowing that accidents happen every day – especially to people who haven't slept much in the last week and not at all in the last thirty-six hours – she worked carefully and methodically. But she wondered, with Scott dying, if she would care if an accident triggered the alarm. If she got infected, she could strip off the ridiculous, cumbersome space suit and work three, maybe four times quicker. It wouldn't matter any more if she came into further contact with that malicious, squirming, invisible piece of string.

She could even hug her son.

It had been four hours and still the phone refused to ring. The doctor said it would take at least four hours. What did "at least four hours" mean? Four hours and four seconds? Five hours? Twenty-four hours? Les sat in the dark and waited for the verdict on his daughter.

It wasn't totally dark. He stared vacantly at the tiny red glow in the corner of the room. The TV was also waiting on standby.

If Charlotte had the sickness, where had she got it from? *Did* she get a gnat bite? Because, if she didn't, perhaps she got it from Christie. And if she got it from Christie. . . What had he done? Christie was out there, beyond the danger zone. Les hadn't wanted to hurt anyone. He'd just wanted to save a champion dog.

He thought that the disease would spread only among those filthy hounds left to roam the streets. He thought that a pampered champion would be immune, untouched by the virus.

Les leapt up when the door bell rang. He virtually sprinted to the front door, turning on the light in the room. On the pavement, there was a man holding up some sort of card. "Sorry to bother you at this—"

"Is it Charlotte?" Les cried.

"Charlotte? No." He held out his warrant card and explained, "I'm a police officer, wanting to ask you a question or two about your dog."

Megan Revill sat on a chair beside her bed and propped up her chin with both hands, resting her elbows on the window sill. She hadn't bothered to close the curtains. She stared intently into the night. She looked studied and thoughtful. But she wasn't. Her head was completely empty. Blank. Thoughts had been obliterated completely by the horror that she had unleashed on the neighbour-hood. Thoughts were too painful, the responsibility too heavy.

In the distance, an army truck came to a halt and its twin brake lights shone boldly red. The colour of haemorrhagic fever.

Once, she had thought that the disease must have come from Tinkers Bridge and would spread only among those filthy houses and streets. She thought that a pampered estate like Passmore would be immune, untouched by the virus. But it wasn't so. She had almost brought life in Milton Keynes to a complete standstill. She had almost brought life to an end.

Chapter 25

Usually, Heather would have ignored the newspaper. This morning, though, Daljit slapped it down in front of her and growled, "What do you think of that, then?"

In huge letters, the front page screamed: DIRTY DOG! Darwin's part in the disease was spelled out in simple vindictive language as if the Revills had done it on purpose. The photograph of the house identified the family for anyone who wanted to vent their anger on a scapegoat. The revelations continued on page two:

Doctor's Own Son in Hospital.
The son of one of the scientists fighting the Milton Keynes plague is himself in

hospital, fighting for his life against the deadly virus. The disease is so destructive to human life that Scott Henman, 17, has been given only hours to live. His mother, university biologist Dr Laurie Henman, has only those few hours to work out a cure. The race is on.

Heather could not read any more. She dropped the newspaper and said to anyone within hearing, "How dare this reporter? It's so . . . intrusive. It's bad enough having the virus to contend with, now we've got a parasite hanging around as well."

While the virus took possession of more and more of Scott's faculties, some reporter was more interested in entertaining the public than with the misfortune of others. Heather wouldn't wish haemorrhagic fever on anyone but she wondered how the journalist would like to be infected while someone splashed her private details across a newspaper in this lurid style.

Scott had lost the battle to communicate. He was in a different, soundless, lonely world of shifting red drapes. Red tide below and above, red skies. Every square millimetre of his skin screamed silently as if he'd been immersed in boiling water. He could tell when Heather topped up his pain killers because, for a while, the excruciating pain became a nagging ache. Sooner or later, usually sooner, the torturers returned and, with glee, lowered him into that dreadful bubbling cauldron again. Yet he accepted it. He was too tired to do anything but lie still and accept it all. He knew that he wouldn't have to put up with it much longer.

The crowd of about twenty angry residents gathered outside the Revills' house. "This is the one!" someone shouted.

Gary Davenport emerged out of the crowd with his trusty aerosol. In huge capitals, he sprayed, "DIRTY" across the door of the Revills' double garage and the mob cheered.

The restless herd chanted, "Passmore filth! Passmore filth!" They were frustrated and furious. Many were the devastated relatives of the dead. Deprived by the hospital's post-mortem procedure of a body, and of a proper farewell with ceremony to express their mourning, they needed to find another outlet for their grief. They needed a different ritual. Each and every one of them knew someone who had died and they needed someone to blame.

Mrs Smith, Tammy's mum, picked up a sizeable stone from the flower bed and hurled it at the large window. It bounced off. But her attack gave them all the same idea. Within a few seconds, stones were bombarding the Revills' window and the glass panels of their front door.

It sounded like gunfire. Stones smacked against the glass. Then one of them crashed right through the lounge window and Megan, flattened in fear against the back wall, screamed.

Rev and Lucy came flying down the stairs.

Aghast, Barry exclaimed, "Where did *she* come from?" He'd had no idea that one of the enemy was in his house.

Freed from restraint by the crisis, Rev said, "She stayed with me last night. I needed company and Lucy was the only one who'd provide it." He looked piercingly at his parents. It was almost an accusation. Then he uttered,

"What's happening? What are you going to do?"

Neither had a reply.

Lucy did not need to ask. She didn't rely on others to do anything. She was used to rolling up her sleeves and getting things sorted out.

At the front door, she ignored the barrage of debris. She opened the door, ducked under a flying stone and put up her hands. "Stop! Stop!" she shouted.

Suddenly unsure, the angry mob hesitated.

On the drive, she pushed up her specs and then adopted her usual stance, hands on hips. She scanned the crowd, noticing that Gary and his uncle were kneeling down, stuffing a rag into a milk bottle filled with a clear liquid, almost certainly petrol. Plainly, the protest was about to get out of control. Someone was about to get killed. "Are you crazy?" she cried. "What are you doing?"

"Getting our own back," someone shouted.

Another voice said, "You know what they done, these people."

"Look," Lucy replied. "You all know me. And I know all you. What you're doing isn't right. These people. . ."

"Traitor!" Gary called. He was remembering

the moment when Lucy had shopped him outside the Hancocks' house.

Another man yelled, "We're goin' to clean up the people who started it all. Like they burn the bodies." He held up the petrol bomb. "This'll clean the place."

"It wasn't the people," Lucy argued. "It was a dog and it's been burnt already. There's nothing here to clean up any more."

"Get out the way, Lucy!"

Lucy stood her ground. "You might as well punish God for inventing gnats. Are you going to burn St Mary's next?"

"They've got to suffer like the rest of us."

"So," Lucy shouted back, "the more that suffer, the better, is it? That doesn't make sense. What are you punishing them for? Ignorance?"

"They killed my Tammy."

"Mrs Smith," Lucy replied. "Would Tammy chuck a petrol bomb into someone's house? Is that what she would've wanted? Maybe if they'd done it on purpose. But how could they know? And Phil," she called to another familiar face in the crowd, "would Oliver have wanted you to do this? I mean, ask yourselves."

The group wavered until Gary yelled

feverishly and desperately, "Face it, they're Passmore people."

"Oh, you're going to torch them because their bricks are fancier than ours! It's not worth it. I mean, we've got far more of a community than they have. We've got more than them. But, I'll tell you, there's a person I like here. I like him because he was brought up to look down on us but it hasn't even occurred to him to do that. He sees everyone – good or bad – for what they are, not for where they live and how much money they've got. No us and them. And there's someone else. Rev's mate, Scott. But he's in hospital. He's going to die today so please don't tell me these people aren't suffering as well. We all taste the same to a gnat or a virus. I won't let you burn Rev's place down. If you do, I'll be in there with him." She turned and strode defiantly back into the house. In the doorway, she shouted, "It's make-your-mind-up time." Then she went inside.

Lucy had spread doubt and chaos among the gang of protesters outside.

Inside, among the glittering fragments of glass, Rev put his arm round her. Barry looked at her and gave her the merest nod of thanks.

For a moment, Rev thought that his mum was going to say something to Lucy or even touch her but she didn't. Like the undead in a horror film, Megan glided past and out through the front door.

At once, the hubbub in the mob died down. They all stared at the grey, lifeless woman walking down the drive. Suddenly, there was no arguing that she was suffering. She seemed to be offering herself as a sacrifice. Megan stopped in front of the crowd and mumbled, "I'm sorry. I'm dreadfully sorry." Then she froze.

Several of the gathering backed away. One or two murmured something incoherent. Mrs Smith stepped forward and asked, "Are you all right?"

In response, Megan collapsed.

Barry dashed towards his wife from the front door. Together with Mrs Smith and Phil Trafford, Barry helped her up and back into the damaged house. Rev brushed aside the glass before they laid her on the sofa.

Mrs Smith and Phil were embarrassed to find themselves in the home that they had nearly destroyed. Even so, before they hurried away, Phil nodded at the broken window, pushed a business card into Barry's hand. Never one to miss a business opportunity, he muttered, "Lowest quotes in the area."

After they'd gone, only the menacing milk bottle remained on the Revills' drive.

Discreetly in the background, Syreeta was still making her notes. Another terrific story had unfolded right in front her. She could hardly believe her luck. When she'd finished, she stepped forward to take a photograph of the abandoned fire bomb.

Gnats: still no samples available
House flies: few samples available; all
*   negative*
Other insects: negative
Bats traced to canal/H9 intersection: area now
*   clean*
Human contacts with potential sources:
*   Charlotte Flynn: positive*
*   Lucy Metcalfe: positive*
Hospital/research staff: still monitoring; all
*   negative except:*
*   Heather Caldbeck: positive*

Chapter 26

Les Flynn had successfully misled the doctor and the policeman who'd come to the door. But now that Charlotte had got the disease, the time for deception was over. He confessed it all to Ross McGavin.

After listening in shock to his distraught parishioner, Ross realized that it was a case for the scientists first and forgiveness second.

Les sobbed, "What should I do? I don't know."

"I'm not an expert, Les, but we *have* to tell the authorities. I suspect your dog could start an infection somewhere else."

"I didn't mean to put anyone else at risk. Especially not Doug. I didn't think. . ."

"Will you come with me to the hospital and tell the scientists?" Ross said.

Les nodded.

"We'll talk on the way."

Looking into the vicar's face, Les asked, "Is Charlotte ill to punish me?"

"No," Ross replied. "I don't think God's got anything to do with this."

When one of Darryl's CDSC colleagues got a message through to the professor inside his protective suit, he swore richly. Turning to Laurie and using the intercom line between them, he said, "I've got to go, Laurie."

"What? But you can't!"

"I'm sorry. I have to."

"What about Scott?"

"There's the possibility of a new outbreak. Containment was always my number one aim. You know it has to be. I have to stop new infections. That comes before . . . exposed individuals."

"But this work. . ."

"Carry on, Laurie. I'll go to this new site, see what's got to be done, leave a deputy in charge and get back as soon as I can. I can't promise any more than that." He headed for decontamination.

Inside the suit, Laurie could not vent her

real feelings. Neither could she wipe the moisture from her eyes. She blinked several times and then tried to continue.

It was only a ten-minute car ride to Stony Stratford, just north of Milton Keynes. Time to make a few quick calls to organize the storming of Doug Flynn's house. There wasn't an opportunity to make the one long call that Darryl really wanted to make. He made it a quick one instead.

When Mark came to the phone, Darryl said, "How you doing? OK?"

"Well. . ." his son began.

"What is it?"

Mark went quiet and there was the sound of a door closing. Then he whispered, "It's Granny's food."

Darryl smiled knowingly to himself. "What about it?"

"She always does cabbage. Yuck."

"Cabbage is good for you, Mark. It's as good as spinach. Makes you grow up like me."

"It tastes like. . ."

"I know, Mark. Remember, I had it for eighteen years. You've only got to put up with it for a few more days."

Darryl's driver was doing eighty. In front of the car, the police escort on motorcycles cleared the road.

"And I got spots. Granny says I might have chickenpox."

"Oh?"

"It can't be right."

"Why not?"

"Because I'm a boy, silly, not a chicken."

Darryl shook his head. He was surrounded by viruses. He explained that boys did get chickenpox, that it wasn't such a bad disease, and that it was best to get it over with while young. "Like the cabbage, it'll only last a few days. With a bit of luck, I'll be back then."

The driver said over her shoulder, "There in a minute."

Darryl rang off and prepared himself for the ordeal.

In the event, the leak could have been a lot worse. Doug had confined the smuggled dog to the house and garden.

"Les told me to keep Christie under wraps," he explained.

"Good. Have you had any visitors?"

"A few. Not many." Doug turned his head to one side and coughed violently.

"We'll need names and addresses." Darryl nodded at his CDSC colleague, indicating that he should write down the details. When Doug had dictated them, Darryl said to his deputy, "OK. Round them up and send them in to the hospital – along with the dog, of course."

"Will we all be OK?" Doug enquired nervously.

"I'm afraid I can't say till we've done some tests. We'll find out later today." To his colleague, Darryl said, "It looks fairly well contained but stay here and supervise, will you? If we get any positives, you'll have to put another quarantine in place."

Doug sneezed and Darryl asked him, "How long have you had this cold?"

"Ages. Can't seem to shake it off."

"From before you took your brother's dog?"

"Yeah."

"Good."

Suddenly, Darryl became silent and thoughtful. Then he yanked out his mobile phone and called the university. When he got connected to Laurie's technician, he said, "Colin, ask Laurie how Scott copes with colds."

After a short wait, the answer came back, "Like he's hardly got them. An enviable immune system. Shrugs them off in twenty-four hours, maximum."

"Right. That's it, then. Thanks, Colin. Tell Laurie to get those T cells ready. I'm on my way with an idea." He rattled off a list of chemicals that he would need. "Got that?"

"I'm on my way to the stores now," Colin replied.

Darryl issued his final orders at speed and then turned to Doug. "Let's get going," he said. "We've got a special van to take you back for a check-up. Have you got a clean glass bowl you can take with you?"

"Bowl? Why?"

"There's something unpleasant I want you to do for me on the way . You see, I'm relying on you for samples of cells contaminated with a cold virus."

Back in the biology department with an unsavoury bowl of saliva and nasal discharges, Darryl said to Laurie, "Here's the plan. We graft Flynn's cells – infected with a cold virus – on to the other end of Scott's killer Ts. When we inject them back into Scott, we know one end will grab his infected cells – we've seen that with our own eyes. The other end will be a standard cold. If he's as good as you say at recovering from colds, it'll bring his white blood cells out in force."

Laurie nodded. "Yes, of course. We link his haemorrhagic fever and a cold into one particle. All his immune system will see is one big foreign object to be attacked. There's a chance he'll have a mutated antibody that'll wipe out the haemorrhagic virus while it's tackling the ordinary cold."

"Exactly. We're going to disguise the haemorrhagic virus as a cold – something we know he's good at fighting."

Laurie's smile faded rapidly. "It's just that . . . I called Heather. He's very poorly, Darryl. We don't have much time. She was upset."

Darryl nodded. "I know. I called as well – from the car. She's upset because of Scott, because Lucy Metcalfe's just been admitted and because. . ."

He hesitated and Laurie saw something in his eyes. Behind the determination, authority and conviction, she saw something new. Anguish. She stammered, "You mean, Heather's positive."

Darryl breathed deeply. "Yes. I was told in the car."

Laurie knew that this brilliant microbiologist and Heather were getting on well but she hadn't realized how far it had gone. She said, "We could speed things up. Because of Scott I'm willing to go in Biolevel 4 and work without. . ."

Darryl interrupted. "No way. Team members come first. You're too valuable, Laurie. Scott wouldn't thank you for sacrificing yourself. Now, let's go and get on with it – fully protected."

The contact with his forehead felt different. Scott opened his eyes and saw Heather through a red haze. Whenever he revisited the real world, his faithful nurse always seemed to be beside him. At first, Scott did not realize why her touch was different. Then it came to him. Her clothing was different, freer. And it was her skin on his brow, not the smooth latex of medical gloves. It could mean only one of two things. Either he was better, no longer infectious, or she was infected with the same virus. His periods of intense pain followed by untroubled calm told him that he was barely alive. He was resigned to his fate but he was sad about Heather. He closed his eyes and thought of her. A small watery drop of blood ran down towards his clogged ears.

Chapter 27

Barry was so used to being bossed about by his wife that he was no longer able to do anything without her say-so. Even when Megan was recuperating in bed. Delicately, Barry mentioned, "We need to get someone in to fix the window. There's a chap called Phil Trafford. The one who helped you inside. He's from. . ."

Megan nodded and pondered on it for a moment. Then, doing her best to smile, she said in an uncharacteristically weak voice, "Give him a call. It's good to give the work to someone local."

Touching his wife's shoulder, Barry replied, "OK. I think, under the circumstances, that's best."

Downstairs, Rev burst in through the front door. "But she can't be infected," he yelled to the empty room. He pointed at the broken window and growled, "She was round here. She was fine."

Charging down the stairs, Barry looked at his son and asked, "Is it Lucy?"

Angrily, Rev retorted, "Since when have you been interested in her?"

"Since this morning. And, I'm sorry, it should have been before."

Rev crumbled, accepting his father's embrace. He whispered, "She's in the early stages, Dad."

Barry nodded. "Then you don't want to be here with us. You want to be at the hospital. Make the most of your time with her, that's my advice. And, Justin, tell her we're thinking of her."

Rev nodded.

Together, Laurie and Darryl stared at the screen. The attachment of Doug Flynn's cells had not been one hundred per cent successful. The electron microscope scanned across free T cells and killer Ts attached to Doug's healthy body cells but, every now and then, there were some attached to body cells that harboured the cold virus.

"Is it enough?" Laurie muttered.

Darryl shrugged. "Only one way to find out. Let's add it to that plate of haemorrhagic cells and see what happens."

A few minutes later, they were back at the monitor. It was a crude, messy experiment. Nothing had been purified. They did not have the time to do it properly, with scientific exactness. The screen showed a jumble of particles. They focused on one particular artificial T cell. It was like a hook dangling in a well-stocked stream. The passing fish were cells corrupted by the bleeding fever. But none of them took the bait.

The two scientists stood side-by-side, leaning over the desk, watching the monitor, begging the free end of the killer T to latch on to one of Scott's passing body cells. After a couple of minutes, Laurie glanced at Darryl with disappointment all over her face. "It's not going to. . ."

"Hang on!" He pointed at the centre of the screen. "Look!"

The two prongs at the end of the altered T cell had clasped a diseased cell. The whole thing looked like two balloons whose strings had got entangled.

"It's working," Darryl said, barely able to whisper in case his optimism was about to be shattered.

They scanned the dish and, every now and then, came across more linked cells.

"It's a hybrid between a cold and haemorrhagic fever," Laurie murmured. She was almost speaking to herself. "It might make Scott's antibodies attack it like they'd go for a trivial cold – or it could be deadly itself."

Through the microphone, Darryl asked Colin for a connection to Heather at the hospital. "How are you, Heather?" he asked anxiously.

"Well, let's look on the bright side. It's a lot easier to look after the patients when I don't have to take all the precautions."

"No, I meant, how are *you*?"

"Coping."

"I wish I could. . . Anyway, I need a realistic, honest opinion on Scott. We've come up with something that stands a chance of working. But we haven't tried it in any experimental animal. We need four to five hours minimum even to do the simplest test with infected mice. Have we got it?"

Heather paused and then gave her verdict. "I don't think so, Darryl. I reckon he's got a couple of hours."

"Two hours!"

"Yes. That's my best guess. He's in a bad way."

"OK. Thanks, Heather. Take care," Darryl responded. "I'll be in touch."

He turned fearfully towards Laurie and gave her Heather's judgement.

Awash with worry and emotion, Laurie cried, "What does she know? She isn't even qualified for this!"

"No, but she cares and she's seen a lot of horrible deaths. She's now our most experienced and reliable nurse."

"There's got to be time to test it in a batch of mice. Infected monkeys would be even better."

"No time, even for the mice," Darryl said firmly.

Laurie replied, "You're asking me to test an unproven medicine on my own son!"

"Yes. I'm asking you to do away with normal medical ethics."

"We've only tested it in a dish. It could do anything in humans. You know that. It could latch on to perfectly healthy cells and instruct his immune system to kill them off. That would be . . . just awful. It could be a killing machine, not a cure at all."

"Yes," Darryl agreed bluntly. He wasn't prepared to provide reassuring and meaningless words. "You're right. It could be the best biological weapon ever made. But it could also trigger a full-scale assault on the virus – if he's got anything of a working immune system left."

Chapter 28

Scott didn't fit his skin any more. He felt that he had shrivelled up inside it. Detached from it, he occupied very little space now. The rest was pure virus. It was like being inside a tent. His inflated skin was the thin material around him. The bright lights out there beyond his skin made it glow crimson except where shadows fell across it. Strange shifting shadows, long and thin. Suddenly, he realized that there were people standing outside the flimsy tent, beyond the virus. Vaguely, he heard voices.

"It's against every ethic in the book," a wretched female voice said. "And it's my own son."

"I've got to be frank," a man said. "It doesn't

matter if it kills him, Laurie. I know that sounds cruel, but he's going to die soon. It's a matter of minutes, an hour at most."

"You don't need to tell me that. I can see for myself! You say we've got a trial cure but we've got a trial poison as well. The cure could be worse than the disease."

"Worse than this?" Heather put in. "Nothing's worse than this. Not even death."

The male voice said, "It's up to you, Laurie, but think about this. The virus is going to kill him without a single hope of recovery. The modified T cells might kill him as well, but they offer hope of recovery."

"One way, nature kills him. The other way, *we* do. That's a big difference. You might be asking a mother to kill her own son. What if it was your lad? Would you give him the injection?"

There was a pause.

"I believe I would, yes. You see. . ."

Suddenly, Heather said, "Shush," and bent down, her ear close to the patient's mouth. If she had not been exposed already, it would have been a ludicrously dangerous act. "He said something," she explained. "I'm sure he did."

Laurie and Darryl thought that it was impossible but they kept quiet anyway.

"I'm listening, Scott," Heather whispered. "Say it again."

Nothing. There could only be silence from a victim at this advanced stage. And the foul breath of death that she had smelled too many times.

Kindly, Darryl said, "You imagined it, Heather. Wishful thinking."

"No!" she insisted. She waved her hand at him dismissively. The muscle in her right arm ached relentlessly and she tried to massage it with her left hand while she waited.

Then there was the merest grunt.

No one within hours of death had been able to say anything but from Scott came a distant moan. It was a voice from deep within him and it was barely audible.

Heather stood upright and the other two stared at her. "Well?" Laurie prompted.

Heather inhaled deeply. "He said, 'Do it.' That's all."

"Are you sure?" Laurie asked.

Heather nodded. "Absolutely sure."

Darryl chipped in, "He can hear us, Laurie! He's given permission."

Laurie let out a long breath. "All right," she said. "But I can't give it to him myself." She looked down at her son and then at the vial, packed in ice. "You make the injection." She gave the package to Darryl and Heather held out a hypodermic syringe. Laurie added, "Just don't mess it up, Darryl."

It felt as if someone had just prodded Scott's tent with a slender spear. It punctured the outer skin, came suddenly through the void and sank into his arm. He opened his mouth to scream but no sound emerged.

Almost as soon as it had come, the weapon was withdrawn from the wound and the pang slowly subsided.

Only one shadow remained. Its voice drifted down to him.

"I hope I did right, Scott. If you *can* hear, I want to tell you I couldn't see another way. I didn't want to make you a guinea pig but it was the only choice. Now – if you were well, you'd like this – you're the most important person in Milton Keynes. All eyes are on you. If you survive this, we can do the same for anyone. Heather, Lucy, all the others who are sick. We can cure it. So don't give up, Scott.

You must be so tired, but try to fight it. I honestly don't believe a clever bit of biochemistry can do anything on its own. I think it's down to you. We've given you a weapon. It's up to you to use it how you will. You see, you can still be the hero."

The shadow stirred uncomfortably. "Do you know what I've always wanted to do? I'd love to see the Grand Canyon. I don't know why. I just like the look of the pictures. But it's always been the wrong time. Too expensive, too near a project deadline, too near GCSEs. But the world's a global village, they say. We could jump on a plane and just go. That's what we'll do when you're better. Jump on a plane – never mind the expense, make it Concorde – and go and take a look at the Grand Canyon. After that, you get to pick a place. What have you always wanted to do, Scott? We'll do it. Promise. We really will. We need time together. Time for ourselves. It's better than worrying about deadlines and exams. And all you've got to do is get well. You're the only patient who's shown the slightest resistance to this virus. You nearly got it. Your immune system had a real good go but it needed a helping hand. That's what we've tried to give it. It's up to you now."

Another pause. "Just remember, whatever happens, I'm really proud of you."

It was like listening to someone speaking in a foreign language. Several phrases were familiar and Scott could translate them into something that made sense. Other sentences floated passed him, an incoherent stream of words. But he got the general idea. Basically, someone out there really cared. And if he battled back to the real world, he wouldn't just cure himself. Somehow, he would cure all the others as well.

Did she say that Lucy was sick as well? Not Lucy, surely. She was too full of life. He would like to think that, if it came down to Lucy versus a virus, the virus wouldn't stand a chance but he knew it wasn't so. And Rev would be heartbroken.

Scott gathered what little remained of his strength and resolve.

"I've got a new job for you," Darryl announced.

"Oh?" Laurie said. Exhausted, she was hoping simply to stay with Scott.

"I need a volunteer to monitor Scott's

progress and report it to me every thirty minutes," he replied. "Are you up for it?"

Laurie smiled. "Thanks, Darryl."

"And I'm not letting you off either," he said to Heather. "I need a blood sample from every infected individual, starting with you. I want you to present yourself to whoever I put in charge of the collection."

"What are you thinking of doing?" Laurie enquired.

"I can't afford to wait and see what happens with Scott. Even if he doesn't respond, it doesn't mean anything scientifically. It doesn't mean the idea's no good. I don't need to tell you that, Laurie. Scott could be too weak to make the engineered T cells work. I need to put the idea through its paces whether he recovers or not. Tests we should've done before trying it on Scott. I want to see what the killer Ts do in exposed mice and monkeys and I need to make more from the serum of other infected people."

"You'll need me to help," Laurie said wearily.

Darryl shook his head. "You stay here. I can enlist a couple of CDSC microbiologists. You've done your bit. Take a rest – and look after Scott."

"Can't you hand it over to your technicians completely?" Heather asked him. "You're running on empty. You need a rest as well."

"Not yet," he answered. "Once I've shown them the procedure, maybe. But right now, I've got a few grams of adrenaline left. You don't have to worry about me when there are more important things to worry about." Tenderly, he smiled at her. Heather looked more than worn – battered emotionally by her experiences and on the verge of serious illness. Darryl realized that he was desperate to stop the virus before her condition worsened. To him, she had become more than just another victim.

Chapter 29

Laurie wished that she was a fairy godmother with a magic wand. She could have waved it over her stricken son and everything would be fine again. But she had only science, not sorcery, on her side. Like the nurses, she was wearing all-over protective clothing and a face mask. She couldn't even break Darryl's quarantine rules, bend down and revive her sleeping prince with a kiss. No fairy-tale ending. A kiss would have been foolish, dangerous, emotional and useless.

Her report after the first half an hour consisted of two words. After an hour, her second update comprised the same two words. "No change."

On the phone, Darryl was upbeat. "No

change is pretty good. No change means no deterioration. Heather thought that he might have slipped away by now."

"No change means no better as well," Laurie remarked.

"He's got a huge infection," Darryl reminded her. "And we've put a drop of medicine in the ocean. It's bound to take him a while to marshal his defences. If he's not getting worse, it's time for optimism, Laurie."

"I don't know what worse would look like."

"I do," Darryl said immediately. "But he's still alive, so there's always a chance."

Before the doctor would allow Rev to see Lucy, she asked him a hundred personal questions about his recent involvement with her. Yes, he'd touched her. No, he hadn't come into contact with her blood. No, she hadn't coughed or sneezed in his presence. But, yes, he had kissed her. Several times. Yes, it was more than a peck on the cheek. Mouth to mouth. With passion, yes. Rev blushed.

"In that case," the doctor said, "you're staying here as well."

Rev smiled. "Oh, good. With Lucy?"

"No. As soon as she was confirmed as infected, we put her in Isolation. We had no choice. You'll be in Observation – for at least four or five hours while we do a blood test."

"I've already had one."

"Have you seen Lucy since the last sample?"

"Lots."

"Then you need another one," the doctor insisted.

"Can I see her, though?"

The doctor sighed but took pity. She nodded. "There's a strict no contact rule for visitors so you'll see her through glass and speak by phone. OK?"

"Thanks," Rev said with enthusiasm.

Lucy was bored. "It's daft," she said. "I feel fine – nothing wrong – but I'm in here with the worst cases."

To Rev, it seemed cruel, like caging a sociable animal in solitude. "Have you seen Scott?"

"No," she answered. "No one round here's saying much. It's like they're holding their breath. I don't know why."

"But he's not. . .?"

"No. They've promised to tell me if the worst comes to the worst." Lucy shook her head and then added, "You know, I've never really needed anyone before. Usually, it's people needing me. That's how it is with me. Now, for the first time in my life, I feel like I could use a bit of help."

"Has your mum been in?"

Lucy nodded. "She's just gone out for a fag. A fat lot of good she is. It's not her fault, though. I mean, what can any visitor do?" She looked directly at Rev.

"I wish *I* could do something."

"How are your folks?"

"Thinking of you."

"Really? You're just saying that."

"No. Dad asked me to tell you. They really appreciated . . . what you did. I think it opened their eyes."

Lucy was amazed. "You mean they're not going to look at me like I'm some slag any more?"

"Definitely not."

"I'm privileged, then."

Rev replied, "It's them that should feel privileged."

* * *

Nature's greatest inanimate sculpture. Nearly three hundred miles long, ten miles wide and up to one mile deep. Spectacular shapes and spectacular colour. Scott imagined himself beside the Grand Canyon, tasting the fresh air, feeling the warmth of the sun on his skin and the wind ruffling his hair. Not a care in the world. The natural colour of the immense gorge was red but each exposed layer had its own tint: grey, green, brown, violet. Way down below him, beyond the crags and ravines, the slate-grey water surged along the rock's vein. Transfixed by the extravagant landscape, Scott watched as a wall of crimson water suddenly appeared at the far end of the valley. The torrent swept along the floor of the gorge, splashing round the tortured rocks, painting everything in its path deep red. He should have been horrified but he wasn't. He was fascinated. It looked frightful but it felt right.

Nature's greatest living sculpture. Miles and miles of arteries and veins gushing with blood. They supplied oxygen and nutrients to every one of his sixty billion cells and took away the waste. They supplied the protein police that patrolled his body, looking for diseased cells.

He should have had thirty trillion blood cells circulating in his rivers but much of the watery fluid had ebbed away. He was weak, his blood count was way down. He was not sure that he still had the energy and resources to let loose a torrent of blood cells but he took a deep breath of air and steeled himself.

Darryl was feeling brighter. Christie the show dog, Doug Flynn and their contacts were all negative. By sheer good fortune, the country had been spared a new outbreak. Charlotte must have been bitten by a gnat after all or caught it direct from another human victim. And Scott was still alive. "He's established a record, Laurie," he said on the phone. "He's our longest surviving patient – easily."

"I don't want a more drawn out death," Laurie retorted. "I want a recovery not an extension."

"Stability has to come before recovery," he replied reassuringly.

"Yeah," Laurie murmured. She was tiring of hearing other people's optimism and words that they thought were uplifting and kind. She wanted to see an improvement with her own eyes. That's what she needed to give her faith.

To change the subject, she asked, "How are your experiments going?"

"Too early to say, but most infected mice injected with modified T cells aren't showing any symptoms yet."

"Really? Not even bleeding noses?"

"Nothing."

"You said, 'most'. What does that mean? How many are dying, anyway?"

Darryl answered, "A lot less than half."

"How many?" she repeated.

"Twenty per cent, roughly."

"Twenty per cent," Laurie said gloomily to herself.

Ever hopeful, Darryl stressed, "Eighty per cent look like they're cured. That's brilliant. And it's early days. I can improve it."

It wasn't early days for Scott, Laurie thought. It would be his last day if he didn't respond to that first, crude attempt at a cure. "Are you trying the same method with Heather's blood cells?" she asked.

"Of course. Both hers and the other patients'. I've got a whole crew of biologists working on it."

"But you're taking personal control of Heather's."

"That's right." Almost defensively he added, "Anyone on the team gets preferential treatment. That's what I've always maintained – from the first day. It's still true."

"I understand."

Laurie really did understand. She would have pushed anyone aside to save her son. Now, Darryl was doing the same for someone else.

Chapter 30

Scott moved. Laurie was sure that he did. Not a lot. Just a leg finding a new position. For that second, he ceased to be an inert body oozing life. And maybe he was leaking less blood. Laurie looked up at Heather.

Heather was nodding slowly, hardly daring to believe the thermometer. "His temperature's headed in the right direction," she said in a whisper, as if premature jubilation might reverse the trend. "And his blood pressure's up a touch. He's retaining more fluid. I need to get the Ward Sister in, Laurie, and probably Darryl or a consultant. This is too important for just me."

Laurie asked, "Have any of the others done this?"

Heather shook her head. "Once they go into the quiet phase, that's it." Unable to be the detached nurse, she blurted out, "I hope it's what I think it is. Please."

Laurie gripped Scott's withered hand. Looking at the caked and blackened blood under his fingernails, she was reminded of the thin hand of a young child who had been playing in mud. She would give everything to feel his fingers close around hers right now. But there was no reaction.

Scott had become incredibly thin. The nurses did not have to weigh him to know that he was wasting away. The distress of moving him was not worth it. And it could have put the staff in danger. Their eyes told them what the scales would have measured precisely. His hair had gone and, no matter how many times he was washed, his body was soon contaminated with blood and sweat.

When the doctor arrived, she was so surprised by Scott's results that she demanded to take the readings herself. And when she got exactly the same figures as Heather had done she hurried away, saying, "I need to speak to Professor Wheeler. We've got to talk about this."

Yet the old man's hand in Laurie's gloved palm remained limp.

Daljit Yusof beamed as she approached Rev. The nurse didn't really need to report his test result. Rev could read it in her face.

"Justin Revill," she announced. "You'll be delighted to know you're in the clear. You're a lucky lad. You didn't pick up the infection from your girlfriend. You can go home."

"Home? No chance. I'm not leaving Lucy."

"Lucy will be with us for quite a while, I'm afraid."

"Aren't you going to warn me there's no cure?" asked Rev glumly.

Daljit leaned close and whispered, "I shouldn't tell you this, but there's a patient about your age who should have died by now. But the doctors gave him something and he might . . . just might . . . be responding."

"Scott?" Rev exclaimed, raising his voice too much.

"Do you know him?"

"Only since I was three."

"Oh, dear," Daljit muttered. "I really should've kept my mouth shut. It's just that it's such good news. We haven't had a glimmer of hope for ages. But don't tell anyone what I told you."

"Why not?"

"False hopes. Counting chickens before they're hatched and all that."

"All right," Rev agreed. "I'll keep quiet on one condition – that you slip word of it to Lucy as well. She's very worried for Scott. And I dare say it'll make her feel a bit better for herself."

It was nearly midnight when Scott shifted his position again. This time it was definite. Both legs and one arm twitched into life before they settled again. Half an hour later, his head moved like someone failing to come out of a deep deep sleep.

Half dozing, half keeping watch, Laurie was startled when she was joined at Scott's bedside by someone not wearing all the gear. "Lucy."

The young woman nodded. She put her hands on her ample hips and examined Scott. "You know, I think he looks better than last time I saw him. A bit more colour."

"You heard, then?"

"I don't think I'm supposed to say but, yeah, I heard. What's going on?"

Laurie told her that, in a sense, they'd made Scott more ill. They had provided him with a second virus – but one that his body would easily defeat. That way, his defences were stirring into action, hopefully destroying the haemorrhagic virus at the same time. Then Laurie asked, "How are you, Lucy?"

"Weird. I mean, there doesn't seem to be anything wrong with me. I haven't even lost any weight. A few little aches and pains, maybe, but that's it. It doesn't seem right to be here in hospital with all the fuss for that."

"Have they told you how the disease progresses?"

"In words of one syllable. Over and over again. I'm waiting for flu in a day or two, apparently."

Suddenly, Laurie caught the sound of the sweetest music that she had ever heard. Not many would have recognized it as music but there it was again. Something between a wheeze and a moan from Scott. It sounded like a dying sigh but ended with a sharp intake like the first breath of a baby. The gasp of new life.

Laurie gasped as well and, with delight in her expression, looked up at Lucy.

To Lucy, it seemed such a little thing. A pitiful groan. "I suppose that's good," she muttered, trying to cheer up Scott's mum.

"He hasn't made a sound for hours." Laurie turned to Scott and said, "It's me. I'm here. And Lucy. She's come to see you."

Of course, there was no response. Yet his bald head lolled to one side and an arm thrashed out, disturbing the cover.

Laurie saw it with her own eyes, she heard the sound with her own ears. Now she could believe in the improvement, even the possibility of recovery. While she rejoiced internally, Lucy turned away.

When Laurie looked up again, she was surprised. "What's the matter?" she said to the girl's back.

Lucy shook her head.

Standing, Laurie said, "What is it?"

"I hate what he's been reduced to. A little while ago he was full of life and now . . . a moan's a major triumph. I mean, that's me in a few days." Upset and irrational, she cried, "I'll have to send Rev home to get my hat."

Laurie took Lucy's shoulders in her protected hands. "If you'd seen him three hours ago, you'd know how I feel. He was virtually dead, Lucy. Now . . . who knows? If he makes it, we'll be doing the same for you well before you get critical. If it works on someone at death's door with hardly an immune system left, the cure'll be much better with a stronger patient who hasn't gone downhill yet. Scott's had to fight back a long way. It'll be much easier for everyone else who's not as ill, whose body defences are still fully functioning like yours. I don't normally predict things but I'll predict this. If Scott continues to improve, and it's a big if, we'll do the same thing with everyone who's infected and they'll all get better before Scott. His journey's so much longer." She decided not to mention that the treatment might fail with some patients.

At last, Lucy turned round. She hid her face on Dr Henman's shoulder. She was getting that overdue bit of help in the form of a sympathetic hug from someone who understood what it was like to be frightened.

Darryl's drained team met in the middle of the night. One chair remained empty. Heather could no longer mix freely with them. They listened to the latest developments with a mixture of satisfaction and scientific scepticism. No one would call for champagne till a patient had been cured, until that person's blood was free of the virus, until he or she could join the celebration. Even so, they wanted to treat all patients as quickly as possible. They wanted all of the remaining victims to be given a chance.

Someone pointed out, "Extracting killer Ts, modifying with another infected cell and re-introducing to the patient, it's a long-winded procedure. And dangerous. Can't be hurried. Not like popping paracetamol. So, who comes after Scott, Darryl? What's the priority?"

Darryl sighed. "This isn't easy, but, until we finish our work here, any infected team member's first in the queue. That's Heather Caldbeck." Once again feeling that he needed further justification, he added, "I've always said we're the most important people. Besides, Heather knows the risks so it's right that she should be the next guinea pig for an experimental medicine – as long as she gives permission. Then, after her, it's got to be those within a day of death – as long as there's a realistic chance they can be saved. After that, all under eighteens. Then other infected adults. Anyone going to object?" He glanced around the assembled faces.

Each one looked down at the table or shook a head.

"All right. Decided," Darryl announced. "I need every microbiologist on the job of generating the preparation – on a voluntary basis, of course, given the hazards."

All of his microbiologists volunteered at once.

A voice called out, "Darryl, do us a favour and take a shave and a shower."

Darryl's hand shot to his stubbly chin. "A shower? I've had so many – in decontamination."

"That's the problem. You smell like a disinfectant factory."

For the first time in days, Darryl laughed.

There was a definite flicker. Once Laurie had wiped the scum from Scott's crusty eyes, he tried again to open them. Only one responded. It was a long-lasting wink.

Scott saw his mother through a haze but it was definitely her. At once, he whispered hoarsely, "The Great Barrier Reef."

"What?" Laurie was so happy that Scott said something that she was almost crying.

"Place to go after the Grand Canyon," he said in a slow, husky voice.

Laurie gripped his arm in both of her hands and let her tears flow. "I never knew you wanted to see that," she sobbed.

"I never said." He felt her grip on his left arm and it hurt only a bit. He coughed violently and grimaced at the pain in his throat. "Thought you'd be too busy. Didn't want to pile on the pressure."

"Oh, Scott, you're a good lad." She wiped her face but the tears would not stop. But these were different, welcome tears. Her shoulders shook and her spine tingled. Blinking and smiling simultaneously, she added, "But you could have picked some-where cheaper."

Chapter 31

Over the next few days, Darryl's more refined treatment was given to all of the patients in turn. And they weren't so different from mice after all. Darryl's results with the experimental animals mirrored the success rate with humans. As Laurie had predicted, the strongest were the quickest to recover. The first to be discharged was Lucy.

Infected individuals:
  Lucy Metcalfe: blood sample now negative

Stubbornly, Rev had occupied the waiting-room, making it his home until he could walk away from the dreadful hospital with her.

Christie and the Flynns would soon

welcome home Charlotte. She had been further down the road than Lucy and took longer to scramble back. But she did.

Infected individuals:
   Charlotte Flynn: blood sample now negative

Scott's return to the real world and to fitness would be an agonizing and protracted haul.

Infected individuals:
   Scott Henman: blood sample still positive
   but virus numbers decreasing dramatically

One of his eyes refused to clear. His vision remained blurred. His fragile legs would not support even his much diminished weight and every one of his joints gave him pain. Food made him sick, the only drink that he could stomach was water. Suddenly inflicted with horrendous migraines, his head felt like a granite boulder balanced on his delicate shoulders. And he wished that he had control over all of his organs. It was so embarrassing. His neck, throat and lungs remained incredibly sore. It was in those places that the infection was most obstinate. Even so, the discomfort of the uphill struggle was worth it. At the summit there was such a prize. A normal life. A miracle.

One young patient was too near to death. Tony, one of the bullies who had tried to force Scott to deposit dog mess through Mr Wishart's letterbox, did not have Scott's resilience. The cure could not yank him back from the edge.

Infected individuals:
Tony Cross: blood sample still positive

And a member of the hospital staff was also going to be part of the tragic twenty per cent. She was not particularly weak, she had hardly reached the flu stage, but the T cell treatment was not rallying her defences. She was going to die from a mixed cold and haemorrhagic virus.

The on-site incinerator was not yet ready to revert to its original task of burning only infected hospital waste.

Amid the relief and rapture, Darryl and Laurie were very hurt. A valued nurse would be killed by their medicine. With his tired head in his hands, Darryl took a deep breath and repeated himself in a troubled whisper, "Eighty per cent cured. It's brilliant. But I *didn't* improve it."

"A week ago," Laurie said, "you'd have settled for fifty per cent, ten per cent, anything."

Darryl looked up and nodded. "Yeah, I know. And I should be used to losing people by now. But I thought I'd seen the last one die. I thought we'd mastered the virus but it's sprung a nasty surprise. I don't like nasty surprises." He sighed again. "It's particularly galling for a nurse to die from a disease she picked up from the people she was tending. It's like a betrayal. She helped them, they killed her. Tragic."

"I'm sorry," Laurie replied in a whisper. There were no other words she could offer.

Infected staff:
Nurse Daljit Yusof: blood sample still positive
Nurse Heather Caldbeck: blood sample now negative

When Rev and Lucy left the hospital hand in hand, Syreeta took a photograph of them and then bounded up to them. "Hello again. How goes it?"

Quick as a flash, Lucy answered, "Well, everything *was* going great."

"Was?" the reporter queried.

"Yes. Scott was well on the road to recovery but someone showed him that newspaper article. He was annoyed. No, he was furious. I mean, no one would want to be splashed across the pages like that. Anyway, he was so upset he went into relapse," she fibbed. "The hospital's crawling with lawyers now."

"Lawyers?"

"It seems they're going to make a case for damages against the journalist." Innocently, she asked, "It didn't happen to be you, did it?"

"Er. . ."

"Oh, dear," Lucy said. "I think you're in trouble. You see, they're saying you're responsible for this new problem. They were talking about suing you for compensation. They mentioned some very big numbers."

Abruptly, Syreeta laughed. "Good try! Nice hoax. You had me worried for a second there." The vulture went back to her lookout by the hospital entrance. But her status as special correspondent was about to come to an end.

Once the barriers around the area came down, the place would be crawling with journalists. She would lose the privilege of being uniquely close to a crisis. She'd return to reporting petty crime statistics, new building projects, domestic disputes and news from schools in the region. Life outside the limelight would never be the same. Alone, Syreeta regretted the passing of the plague.

Chapter 32

Daljit had died and her body had been burnt. She was the last. Scott was still poorly but no longer infected. There had not been any new victims for eight days – the incubation period of the disease. The army had decamped. Darryl had held his final meeting with his Milton Keynes team. He'd thanked them, opened some bottles of wine with them and drunk to the conquest of the enemy. Once they'd observed a minute's silence for Daljit and all of the other casualties, the meeting became a party. Heather was guest of honour, pampered by everyone, especially by Darryl. But for five minutes Scott Henman was the star. Laurie wheeled him into the celebration and everyone in Darryl's team rose to their feet spontaneously and cheered. When the ovation died down, Scott even managed to say a few words of thanks through his embarrassment, elation and fragility.

With a wink, Darryl gave his best patient a small drink of wine and said, "It'll do you good. Just don't tell your mum."

Heather put a hand on Scott's arm and said fondly, "It's great to see you out of the ward, getting back to health." She pointed to the top of his head and added, "You're even getting a bit of hair back."

In his rasping voice, Scott replied, "It's good to see you out of Isolation as well. I . . . er . . . owe you a lot. Thanks for . . . everything." Before his emotions got the better of him in front of everyone, he asked for his mum to take him back. Besides, the brief excursion had exhausted him.

Afterwards, alone with Darryl at home and with a little too much alcohol in her blood, Heather dared to breathe, "Is it really over? I can hardly believe it."

Darryl took her by the shoulders. "I haven't been able to do this before." He leaned into her and kissed her passionately. Then he said, "Yes. It's over."

She smiled, keeping her eyes closed. "Our job together's over, then." There was also regret in her tone.

"Yes."

She looked at him and said quietly, "You go home – back to Mark – and I get on with normal work."

Darryl shook his head. "I've already had a word with the hospital. After what you've been through, compassionate leave is the least you get. You need a break – and some help. If you wanted, you could come and stay with me for a while. That way, I return the favour."

"Don't tell me: you're brilliant at psychology as well. You're going to supply post-trauma therapy."

"No. Just a friend if you need one."

Heather nodded. "Yeah, I could use a friend."

"So you'll come?"

"What about Mark? He'll want you to himself for a while."

"I got the impression he was looking forward to meeting you. Said you had a nice voice on the phone." Darryl asked, "Ever had chickenpox?"

With a puzzled expression, Heather

laughed. "Sure. When I was this high." Her hand wavered around about knee height. "Why?"

"You'll be all right, then. He's got chickenpox so he'll need cheering up. You'll help me do it. Won't you?"

Heather hesitated and then hugged him tightly. "Why not?" she whispered in his ear. "I'd love to."

Chapter 33

Ross McGavin still had a duty to perform. His role had not ended once the restrictions had been lifted. Afterwards, consolation and comfort were needed more than ever. He'd set himself the task of visiting every household in the neighbourhood. Nearly done, he was traipsing through Woughton Park, trying again the few homes where he had not got a response before.

Aaron Wishart was a pale individual. Spending nearly all of his time out of the sun, he normally looked sickly even though he was squeaky clean and apparently healthy. But his obsession with hygiene had left him danger-ously weak. He had lived in such sterile conditions that his immune system was weak. In his barren germ-free world, he'd given it no work to do for years and it had forgotten how to function. When he'd opened his inner door to check that the outside door had been mended satisfactorily, he'd been bitten by an infected gnat that the repairer had let in to the porch. Aaron's disused immune system could not even manage token resistance to the virus that the insect injected into him. He could not cheat death by isolating himself after all.

The house was eerily quiet. In the spotless bathroom, the antibacterial soap and antibacterial sponge had hardened through lack of use and moisture. There was no movement in the kitchen. The antibacterial cutting-board was tucked away in its clean polythene bag. There were no scraps of food on the stainless surfaces. The computer lay dormant in the empty study and the television in the lounge was dark and silent. The toilet, unflushed for days, smelled strongly of bleach. The spare bedrooms were un-occupied, the beds stripped down. Aaron did not expect, and did not invite, visitors.

Aaron Wishart himself was no longer pale. He lay on his bed upstairs, darkened skin stretched like parchment over prominent bones, on his antibacterial sheets. Brown blood had run from every orifice of his head and clung to his face like solidified wax to a candle. Clumps of his hair were adhering to his antibacterial pillow and his crumpled antibacterial quilt was caked with black blood. No human being had died so slowly and so painfully of haemorrhagic fever since Yombe's father had perished in Zaire. No human being had died so alone.

At the last house Ross did not get an answer on the entry phone and there was no reaction to his banging on the door. He was about to walk away when some instinct told him not to. He shuddered, unable to turn his back on the deserted house. It was as if he'd sensed an evil spirit that he had to confront. Something was very wrong. Swallowing his nerves, he lifted the flap in the door and peered into the porch. Nothing. There was a smell, though. A smell that revolted him. At once, he felt sick. Grimacing, he murmured, "Ugh!" He tried to force open the door but it would not budge. Instead, he went to get help. The next door neighbour forced the blade of his spade into the newly repaired door and yanked on it, shattering the wood all over again. The outer door sprang open.

The internal door was not locked. When Ross pushed it inwards with a tentative hand, foul air engulfed him. For a moment, he closed his eyes and winced. It was the devil's smell. Utterly evil. Ross put a handkerchief to his mouth and stepped into hell.